# "Fifty thousand pounds sterling."

"That was the amount Damien owed my family," Kassim continued blandly. "When I went over to England to collect it, he couldn't come up with the cash. Your ex-lover offered you to me instead. The man is a fool, Janene. You're proving to be more of a bargain than I thought."

**ALEX RYDER** was born and raised in Edinburgh, Scotland, and is married with three sons. She took an interest in writing when, to her utter amazement, she won a national schools competition for a short essay about wild birds. She prefers writing romantic fiction because at heart she's just a big softie. She works now in close collaboration with a scruffy old one-eyed cat who sits on the desk when she doesn't get it right, but winks when she does.

# ALEX RYDER

## The Barbarian's Bride

## Harlequin Books

TORONTO • NEW YORK • LONDON
AMSTERDAM • PARIS • SYDNEY • HAMBURG
STOCKHOLM • ATHENS • TOKYO • MILAN
MADRID • WARSAW • BUDAPEST • AUCKLAND

ISBN 0-373-18635-5

THE BARBARIAN'S BRIDE

First North American Publication 1996.

Copyright © 1995 by Alex Ryder.

This edition published by arrangement with Harlequin Books S.A.

® and TM are trademarks of the publisher. Trademarks indicated with
® are registered in the United States Patent and Trademark Office, the
Canadian Trade Marks Office and in other countries.

Printed in U.S.A.

# CHAPTER ONE

IT WAS the usual kind of party—too noisy, too over-crowded, too smoky—and she could feel the beginnings of a headache coming on. Right now she was standing by the French window, alone, feeling awkward and wishing that she was back in her own comfortable flat curled up on the settee with a cup of cocoa and a good book. The glass of champagne in her hand was warm and flat and she surreptitiously hid it behind the nearby cheese-plant, then looked around in quiet desperation for some sign of Damien. He'd promised that he'd only be gone for a minute or two but she'd had to fend off, politely but firmly, two advances already. It looked as if it was the open season on green-eyed redheads.

Suddenly there was a man's voice in her ear, enquiring softly, 'Miss Janene Peters?'

Oh, no! Not again! This would be the third. And they were even going to the trouble of finding out her name first. She longed for the safety of her flat even more.

She turned to look at the man who'd spoken, but the rebuff forming on her lips died as her mouth went dry. For a moment she could only wonder at the odd feeling of apprehension that sent a tingle down her spine. Recovering quickly, she offered him a bland smile and arched her brows questioningly. 'Yes. That's me.'

He held out a hand and smiled. 'We've never met, but don't be alarmed. I'm not quite as disreputable as I look. Allow me to introduce myself. My name is Kassim Riffik.'

His fingers were long and tapering and his handclasp firm and cool, and again she felt that inexplicable tingle. He didn't look like the type who went on the prowl for casual pick-ups. Tall, at least six feet two, he had the lean, dark and hungry look that would have kept most women awake at night. His complexion was the dark olive she associated with sun-scorched deserts, his thick hair raven-black and his eyes the most startling blue she'd ever seen, hard and brilliant as sapphires. Beneath a thin straight nose his mouth was wide and there was a suggestion of cruelty in those thin lips, although they were now drawn back in a friendly smile to reveal perfect white teeth. His suit of dark silk and his dazzling white shirt were handmade to accentuate the wide shoulders and slim hips.

'May I get you a drink, Miss Peters? Something a bit more palatable than the one you've so cleverly disposed of.'

His voice was deep and resonant and his English tinged with a faint French accent. Aware that she'd been staring at him in awestruck silence for the last few seconds, she gathered her scattered wits together and stammered, 'No—no thanks. It's very kind of you but I—I'm waiting for my fiancé. He—he should be here at any moment.'

His gaze slid over her with slow and deliberate provocation, lingering for far too long on the amount of cleavage visible over her low-cut dress, and every nerve in her body twitched like a nervous candle-flame. Finally he drawled with quiet amusement, 'Damien will be here shortly. I believe he's involved in some kind of business deal with one of his clients. As a matter of fact, it was he who suggested that I keep you company until he can rejoin you.'

Her face and voice were suddenly stiff with embarrassment. 'Oh. . . I see. . . Did—he say how long he'd be?'

In spite of his expression of sympathy there was a hard edge of irony in his voice. 'No longer than necessary. I'm sure he misses every precious moment of your company.' His blue eyes regarded her innocently, then he made an eloquent gesture with his hands. 'Of course, I've no wish to impose my unworthy presence where it isn't wanted. If you'd rather be on your own. . .'

She could recognise a piece of subtle manipulation as well as the next person. If she rejected his offer she was guilty of discourtesy, to say the least. On the other hand, if she accepted his offer, then, by implication, she wanted him to stay. The truth was that he was making her more nervous by the minute, but she could hardly tell him that without making a fool of herself. In spite of his expensive clothes and the veneer of civilisation, it wasn't too hard to imagine him bare-chested, sword in hand, engaged in an orgy of rape and pillage.

Wondering if she was in danger of becoming paranoid, she said primly, 'It's thoughtful of Damien and very obliging of you, Mr Riffik.'

He grinned. 'The pleasure is all mine, Miss Peters. . . or may I call you Janene? It's much friendlier. You don't mind, do you?'

Her mouth was going dry again and she gulped. 'N—not in the least.'

'Good.' The white teeth flashed in another broad

smile. 'Then you must call me Kassim.' Reaching past her, he deftly opened the French window, then took her by the elbow. 'Let's step outside. It's much quieter and cooler on the balcony.'

A moment later, wondering why the thought of resisting had never even entered her head, she found herself outside, high above the late-night traffic of West London. Across the buildings to the south she saw the lights of Chelsea Bridge in the distance. Overhead, a jet, landing-lights piercing the thin clouds, thundered towards touch-down at Heathrow.

His hold on her elbow was light yet electrifying, and she swallowed nervously. There had been a time when she would have known how to deal with a situation like this. She might even have treated the whole thing as a joke and laughed it off. She might even have flirted with him a little, but those days were gone. The only things she wanted out of life now were stability and security, and she already had those with Damien. Marriage to Damien was going to be her salvation and anything that threatened it was a hazard to be avoided at all costs.

'Have—have you known Damien for long?' she ventured awkwardly.

He gave a slight shrug. 'We know each other through our mutual business interests. It's because of him that I'm paying this all-too-short visit to London.'

'I see. . .' It sounded plausible enough. Damien seemed to know so many people and he was forever introducing complete strangers to her. It was impossible to remember them all. She had no reason to doubt this stranger's story but, if that predatory grin on his face was suddenly translated into action, she could easily side-step him and dash through the window back into the anonymity of the crowd.

'And now we'll talk about you, Janene,' the dark stranger murmured softly. He reached for her hand and glanced at her engagement-ring. 'Damien tells me that you're to be married soon. How long have you known each other?'

'We—we met six months ago,' she answered haltingly, wishing he would talk about something else.

He stepped closer and, with her back to the balustrade and his body between her and the window, there was no chance of escaping. 'How old are you, Janene?'

Right now she felt like a very nervous seven-year-old, but she answered shakily, 'Twenty-four.'

His face was hovering over hers like a hawk over a helpless rabbit. Those blue eyes seemed to impale her, making her incapable of movement as he raised a hand to finger her thick red tresses. 'You are breathtaking in your beauty,' he whispered in a soft, husky voice. 'In my country, such a desirable woman as you would have been a bride at sixteen. Lovers would have begged for a kiss from those sweet red lips. Men would have fought like tigers over you. Gold, silver and precious jewels would have been yours for the asking. . .flowers strewn at your feet.' He paused, and studied her expression with amusement. 'Ah! You are embarrassed and you think I am too effusive in my praise of your charms?' He gave a throaty chuckle. 'I know all about English women. Cold and remote and suspicious of anyone south of Dover. Breeding inhibits the true expression of their feelings.'

Her heart was thudding in her ears and she could feel herself being drawn under by those compelling blue eyes. With an effort she tore her mesmerised gaze from his, but his soft voice continued to provoke and inflame her.

'It merely increases a man's pleasure to strip the shell of cold reserve away bit by bit and release the storm of fire and raging passion beneath the surface. And there is a fire in you, Janene. I sense it. A raging volcano, ready to. . .' Suddenly he spread his hands and heaved a sigh. 'But I forget myself. A thousand pardons. You are promised to another. If it were to anyone other than my good friend, Damien, I would steal off with you in the night and take you to my tent, and there, under the stars, we would lie in each other's arms and. . .'

She chanced a quick glance into those dangerous eyes and smiled in spite of herself. 'Tent? Did you say tent?'

'A mere figure of speech,' he admitted with a crooked grin. 'Some day you will see my humble abode. . . Well, it's not that humble. Quite luxurious, in fact. I'm sure you'd be favourably impressed. You and Damien must be my guests some time.'

His display of dry humour made him seem just a little less threatening, and she murmured, 'I'm afraid that you'll have to ask Damien about that.'

He inclined his head. 'But of course. It is always up to the man to make the decision and it is the woman's place to defer to his wishes in all things. However, I'm sure he couldn't deny you anything you've really set your heart on. He loves you greatly, is it not so?'

She detected something beneath the bantering tone— a subtle edge of interrogation—that once again put her on her guard. 'He wants to marry me,' she answered firmly. 'I think that should answer your question.'

There was a moment of silent tension between them, then he gave a thin smile. 'Yes. He would be a fool not to love a woman such as you. And since you've known him for six months and accepted his ring as a token of your promise, I can only assume that you reciprocate that love.'

She swallowed. 'I'd never dream of marrying a man I wasn't in love with.'

'Of course not,' he murmured. 'And I'm sure you've thought long and deep about it——'

'It's getting chilly now,' she interrupted prudently. 'I'd like to go back inside now, if you don't mind.'

He gallantly removed his jacket and draped it over her bare shoulders. 'In a moment. Meanwhile, this will keep you warm.'

She could feel his body-heat on the material, and the protest she had been about to make died on her lips and her eyes fell away in confusion.

Her passive acceptance of the situation seemed to please him, and he said huskily, 'You don't belong with that crowd in there, Janene. A garden of weeds is the wrong setting for a rose.'

He leaned closer, and for a terrified moment she was certain that he was going to sweep her in a crushing embrace and kiss her. Would she have the strength or the will to resist? And, if she didn't, would he take it as permission to go even further?

'Look. . .' she said, near to panic, 'I—I don't think that Damien had this in mind when he asked you to—to look after me.'

His dark eyebrows arched upwards, mocking her feeble protest. 'Had what in mind? Surely it would please him to know how much I approve of his taste in women. He would surely take it as a compliment. Anyway, I'm sure he's not the jealous type.'

He was just playing with words now. . .not to mention her feelings and peace of mind. 'Well. . .just stop all this talk about how—how beautiful I am.' She nodded in the direction of the window. 'There are plenty of women in there a lot more glamorous than I am. There's nothing special about me.'

'Damien thinks there is,' he countered smoothly. 'When he told me about you he became quite lyrical. So lyrical, in fact, that I put it down to over-zealous exaggeration. Now, however, I can see that he didn't do you sufficient justice.'

His persistent flattery was wearing away at her defences and she couldn't deny the fact that her heart was beating faster than normal, nor that she was starting to feel light-headed. But then, a woman would have to be an unfeeling lump of clay not to be overwhelmed by that potent blend of polished charm and raw sex appeal.

Pulling herself together and trying to keep a firm grip on reality, she diverted the talk towards safer ground. 'You said that you'd come to London to see Damien. Are you and he in the same kind of business?'

For some reason he seemed to find that suggestion amusing. 'Not really, Janene. You could say that fate has caused our paths to cross.'

She kept the conversation going. 'I see. And what exactly are your interests, Kassim?' She'd never yet met a successful man who could resist the temptation to talk about himself, and she didn't suppose that he'd be any different.

His blue eyes glittered and there was another flash of

white teeth. 'At the moment, my interest is in an enchanting woman with hair like the setting sun and eyes the colour of emeralds.'

Oh, God! she thought. Why was Damien taking so long? 'I was referring to your business interests,' she said with quiet reproach. 'I just wondered what you did for a living.'

'Oh, this and that,' he said airily. 'I have a few acres of poor land. Some camels, sheep and goats. I manage to scrape by.'

She fingered the material of the jacket around her shoulders and said drily, 'That's hard to believe, Mr Riffik. People who "scrape by" can't afford Italian silk suits.'

'Expensive clothes. . .' he murmured. 'My only vice.'

She doubted that very much, but had no intention of probing any deeper. He had the look of a man who was used to walking through the darker alleyways of life and emerging unscathed.

'Where exactly are these few acres of poor land?' she asked, determined not to let him hijack the conversation again.

His eyes were fixed appreciatively on her cleavage again, and he shrugged and said dismissively, 'Morocco. A little country in the north-west corner of Africa. Right next door to Algeria. Perhaps you've heard of it?'

'Yes. . .' she murmured with mild sarcasm. 'I did do geography at school.' She racked her brains now and wished she'd paid more attention to her lessons. Morocco. . . Mountains and deserts. . . Casablanca. . . 'Play it again, Sam'. . . Marrakesh!. . .the Marrakesh express—wasn't that a song? And there was Fez! Was that a city or a funny red hat? She knew that a kasbah was a fort and that a souk was a market. And that was about the sum total of her knowledge about Morocco.

'I always thought that Morocco belonged to France,' she said, trying to sound intelligent.

His lips stretched in a smile. 'The French, Portuguese, Spanish—even the Romans. Throughout history many nations have tried to impose their will on us but now at last our country belongs to its rightful owners. The Berbers. Or, as the Romans called us, the barbarians.'

She wasn't the least bit interested in history or politics, but she managed a fair impression of a student thirsting for knowledge. 'Barbary!' she said suddenly. 'The Barbary Coast! Pirates! I saw a film about it once.'

He laughed mockingly. 'Praise Allah! You saw a film about it. Ah, where would we be without Hollywood? But you're quite right, Janene. Corsairs came from Morocco. Your ancestors knew us very well. Our ships roved north as far as England. Women and children would be snatched from their beds at night and taken back to be sold as slaves.' His hand came up and his long fingers gently caressed her cheek. 'A woman like you would have fetched a king's ransom.'

Her mouth was drying up again and a pulse was fluttering in her throat. The mental image she'd had of him as bare-chested with sword in hand hadn't been far off the mark after all. That was exactly what he reminded her of: a dangerous pirate! With a heavy gold ring in his ear and a pointed beard, he'd look the part perfectly.

'Of course,' he went on in a tone of regret, 'civilisation has caught up with us at last. The authorities won't tolerate such behaviour in these enlightened times. They've taken all the excitement out of life.'

'Thank God for that!' she said drily.

'Hmm. . .' His blue eyes gleamed with wicked amusement, then he murmured, 'I imagine there are more than a few women in this cold land who wouldn't object too strenuously if someone snatched them from their beds and took them to a warmer clime.'

'We have tour operators for that kind of thing these days,' she retorted. 'Anyway, what's wrong with the women in Morocco? Aren't there enough to go round?'

He leaned down slightly, until his lips were only inches from her ear, and she felt the moist warmth of his breath as he whispered, 'For men who have an insatiable desire for beauty, there never seem to be enough. But with a woman like you to share his life, a man could ask for nothing more.'

Her heart was palpitating and her legs felt weak, but she found the strength to raise her palms and push them hard against his chest. Enough was enough! It was time she began asserting herself and putting this brazen rogue in his place. 'Now, look here, Mr Riffik. . .I don't like the way you're——'

'Kassim,' he whispered seductively in her ear. 'Mr Riffik sounds far too formal. I would rather have our relationship on a more. . .intimate level.'

She pushed even harder and gasped, 'I know you would! You're making your intentions all too obvious. Now, will you please step back and give me room to breathe?'

He straightened up and gave a mock smile of contrition. 'Please forgive me, Janene. You find the prattling of my foolish tongue disturbing. But please do not be alarmed. I would sooner be cooked slowly to perfection over a bed of hot charcoal than see any harm come to you. I would rather be cast naked into a pit of scorpions——'

'All right!' she said in exasperation. 'Don't make a meal of it. If it wasn't for that look in your eyes I might be tempted to believe you.'

He shrugged and spread his hands in a gesture of supplication. 'My eyes can only mirror the beauty they behold.'

Her green eyes glittered at him angrily. 'Dammit! You're doing it again!' For a moment she wondered if Damien had put him up to this for some sort of gag, then she instantly rejected the thought. Damien would never dream up such an outrageous idea.

'Look,' she said with patient resignation. 'You're simply wasting your time with me, Kassim. You're a very attractive man, I'd be lying if I—if I said I wasn't pleased that you also find me attractive. . .'

'Not just attractive. Positively alluring,' he said with a grin.

'But,' she went on, ignoring the remark, 'this ring on my finger means a lot to me. There's only room in my life for one man, so if you're looking for someone to seduce I suggest you go back inside and find someone more susceptible to your charms.'

He contemplated her in a thoughtful silence which dragged and stretched her nerves. 'So,' he said at last. 'You don't object to me personally. It's simply the fact that you've promised yourself to Damien?'

'No,' she was forced to admit, ruefully. 'I've nothing against you as a person. As I said, you're quite attractive.' She paused, then added drily, 'A fact I'm sure you're well aware of. On the other hand, you're rather egotistical, but then, most men are as a rule.'

He stroked her cheek again with a long finger and gave vent to a sigh of desperate longing. 'Ah. . .if only you would come with me to Morocco, Janene. I would drive every thought of any other man out of your mind.'

'Yes,' she replied tartly, 'I'm sure you'd try your best, but don't hold your breath. There's as much chance of me going to Morocco as to the far side of the moon.'

'One should never challenge the fates,' he cautioned with a cynical smile. 'We may meet again sooner than you think.'

Something in his eyes made her look away quickly and she made a mental note to stick to Damien's side like glue from now on. If he had to meet clients in private, she was going to lock herself in the loo until it was safe to come out again.

'I'm going inside now,' she announced firmly.

His finger had traced its way lightly to the skin below her ear, sending tiny tremors through her nervous system. Reluctantly he straightened up and slid the jacket from around her shoulders. 'I don't think Damien realises how lucky he is, Janene,' he murmured softly. 'When you and I meet again there will be nowhere to run to. We'll be alone. And then we'll see what kind of a woman you really are beneath that shell.' Taking her gently by the arm, he led her back inside.

'So what did you think of Kassim, then?' Damien asked, when he finally turned up to reclaim her a few minutes later.

She clung to Damien's arm and stared after Kassim as he departed and disappeared into the crowd. 'I—I don't know,' she stammered. 'He's a bit overpowering. I'm still trying to get my breath back.'

Damien grinned. 'So he made a pass at you? I'd have been annoyed if he hadn't. It's his way of paying you a compliment. You know what these hot-blooded Mediterranean types are like.'

'No, I didn't. But I do now.'

Damien didn't seem interested in pursuing the subject, and as he started leading her towards the bar she pulled him up. 'I don't want another drink, darling. I think I'd rather rather go home.'

He looked at her in surprise, then glanced at his watch. 'It's still early. I've got another client to meet in half an hour.'

She gave him a weary smile. 'Don't worry about me, darling. I know how important your clients are to you. You stay and I'll get a taxi home.'

'No. I wouldn't dream of it!' he said indignantly. 'You stand right here while I fetch your coat.'

She restrained him once more. 'You're going to make me feel guilty. The fact is that I've got a bit of a headache. I need an early night for a change. You stay here and enjoy yourself.'

He frowned. 'I'm not here to enjoy myself, Janene. I hate these damn parties, if you want to know the truth. But mine isn't a nine-to-five job. Really important deals aren't done in offices. . .'

She soothed his ruffled feathers with an understanding smile. 'I know, I know. They're done over expense-account lunches and at social events and parties like this. But you'll never get rich standing here talking to me. Now, just phone for a taxi while I go upstairs and get my coat.'

He looked at her uncertainly for a moment, then he kissed her on the cheek. 'You're a girl in a million, Janene. I'll make all this up to you when we get married.'

Thirty minutes later she was back in the peace and quiet of her flat. After a shower, she wrapped herself in a bath-robe and settled down in front of the electric fire with a hot, milky drink.

Her encounter with Kassim had left her feeling tense and jumpy, and when the phone suddenly rang she almost leapt off the settee in agitation.

'Hi. How's the headache?'

She relaxed at the sound of Damien's voice. 'Still there. I've taken a couple of aspirins.' There was a lot of background noise. 'Did you meet your client?'

'Yes. And now I'm leaving.' He hesitated a moment, then went on hopefully, 'Would you like me to drop round? I can fill your hot-water bottle. Fetch your teddy.'

She smiled to herself. Damien wasn't a demanding lover. He was considerate, and sex provided them with mutual satisfaction. It could be the very therapy that she needed right now. 'Well. . .it sounds like a wonderful idea, darling,' she murmured. 'But I really am tired. And I wouldn't want to fall asleep in the middle of you-know-what.'

'Yeah. . . That would really put a dent in my pride.' His voice was filled with wry amusement. 'In that case, I'd better not take the chance.'

Feeling that she had somehow to make it up to him,

she suggested quietly, 'Perhaps tomorrow? We can stay in. I'll make dinner and get some wine.'

'Sorry, darling. It sounds great, but I won't be able to make it.' There was a genuine note of regret in his reply. 'I'm leaving first thing in the morning. I have to go north for a few days on business and I won't be back till Saturday.'

Her heart sank. Everything seemed to be going wrong. First that dark stranger with his thinly veiled threat, and now the prospect of being left on her own for the best part of a week.

Damien's voice came again, cautiously optimistic. 'I thought it would be a good idea if you went down to the cottage in Kent. It would give you a chance of a rest. I can drive straight down there and join you on Saturday. Then we can spend the following week together.'

She immediately brightened up. 'That's a brilliant idea, darling. I'll pack a few things and leave the day after tomorrow.'

They spoke for a few more minutes, discussing details, then she hung up. Finishing her drink, she went to the window and peered down into the darkened street below. Finally, satisfied that there was no one remotely looking like Kassim Riffik hanging about in the shadows, she drew the curtains, put the safety-chain on the door and went to bed. All right, she told herself firmly, perhaps she was being childish—but there was no sense in taking any chances.

# CHAPTER TWO

IN THE morning, over breakfast, Janene made up her mind to leave for the cottage that very day. There was no point in staying here alone with nothing to do. If she went down today she could give the place a good clean and airing, and perhaps do a bit of decorating before Damien arrived.

But first there was the lunch-date with Sally. She wasn't looking forward to it, but she didn't like breaking promises. It wasn't that she had anything against Sally. They'd been the best of friends, as well as being business partners, in the past. But it was the past she was trying to forget, and a meeting with Sally would only resurrect buried memories and guilt.

She tidied the flat, changed from jeans and sweater into her favourite pale cream linen suit, then packed her suitcase. Finally she locked up the flat, then went downstairs and put her suitcase in the boot of her car. Knowing the futility of trying to find a parking space in the West End, she left the car in the mews garage and went in search of a taxi.

The Red Candle Grill and Bar had been a favourite haunt of theirs in the old days, and as her eyes got used to the subdued lighting she saw that the place hadn't changed much.

Neither had Sally. Still the same restless, youthful energy, although she had to be in her late twenties by now. Still the same mass of tight, black curls, and large, pink-framed glasses. She was wearing a smartly cut business suit in charcoal-grey and at the moment she was somehow managing to look pleased and slightly annoyed at the same time.

'So what's the matter?' she demanded as Janene settled herself opposite. 'Have I got the plague or something? Four times I phoned last week and four times you said you were busy. We're old friends, right? Old friends should never be too busy for a chat and a meal together.'

Janene lowered her eyes and murmured, 'I'm sorry. Things have been a little hectic lately.'

'Hmm. . . Busy social life, eh?'

The scepticism in the voice made her wince. She should have known better than to try to fob Sally off with a lie. Sally was too perceptive.

Sally tossed the menu across the table. 'I'm having the veal.'

'Then I'll have the same. I hope it's as good as it used to be.'

'It is. Take my word for it.' Sally beckoned a waiter, gave the order, then settled back in her seat with her martini. 'Aren't you going to ask me how the business is doing?'

She smiled. 'Of course. How are things?'

'Huh!' Sally snorted. 'I wish you hadn't asked, but since you have I'll tell you. I'm standing on tiptoes and the water is up to my chin.' She sighed and shrugged. 'It's tough for everyone in this damned recession. I shouldn't complain. At least I can still afford to eat here.' She laughed. 'Do you remember the greasy-spoon we used to eat in up in Camden?'

Janene nodded and felt a tug of nostalgia for the old

days. Camden, in North London. That was where it had all started. . .

They'd first met while browsing around the stalls in the street-market, and they'd taken an instant liking to each other. Over coffee and hamburgers in a café, they'd bemoaned the limited choice of goods on offer in the market and had decided there and then to go into business for themselves. They'd pooled their capital and opened a stall specialising in unusual costume jewellery and accessories. Within two years they'd owned a string of boutiques across London.

In those days she'd been just as single-minded and aggressive as Sally, and they'd carved their way to success through a hostile world of reluctant bank managers and cut-throat competitors.

In her case, at least, the real reward hadn't been the money but the feeling of independence and accomplishment. Much to the consternation of her staid and rather old-fashioned parents, she'd always rebelled against the idea that it was a man's world, and a woman's role was to settle down and be a good little housewife.

They had been pleased about her success, of course, but she had sensed their underlying disappointment. They had wanted grandchildren, but their only child was more interested in a career than motherhood. She hadn't even had a boyfriend—at least none she cared to date on a regular basis.

It had been guilt just as much as a spirit of generosity that had prompted her to treat them to a month's holiday in Florida, all expenses paid. And it had probably been a wish not to hurt her feelings that had made them accept.

She'd driven them to Heathrow, hugged them both,

told them to have a wonderful time and not forget to write, and then watched as the jet thundered down the runway and rose gracefully into the air. . .

'I want you back in the business with me.'

Sally's voice broke into her thoughts and she blinked. 'What?'

'I want you back in the business,' Sally repeated impatiently. 'We can come to some agreement right now. Come on, Janene. What do you say? We were a great team once. We can do it again.'

The waiter arrived with the meal and Janene heaved a mental sigh of relief. 'Let's eat first and give me time to think about it,' she prevaricated.

Resuming her career was the last thing in the world she intended doing, but she hated the thought of letting Sally down. It had been the realisation that something like this might happen that had made her reluctant to come in the first place.

Respecting her wishes, Sally didn't pursue the matter until they were having coffee, then she asked abruptly, 'Well? Have you thought about it? Do we have a deal or not?'

All through the meal her mind had been grappling with the problem, and now she said, 'I'd like to help you all I can, Sally. If you're going through a bad patch, I'd be glad to help out financially. You only need to ask.'

Sally eyed her in frustration, then, in her usual straightforward manner, got straight to the point. 'That isn't the reason for this meeting, Janene. You're the one that needs help, not me. It's been a year since that—that terrible accident. You should be over it by now. You can't let it affect your whole life.'

'I—I don't know what you're talking about,' she muttered into her cup.

'Of course you do!' Sally said in irritation. 'You keep blaming yourself and that's silly. You've put your head under the blanket and you're determined to keep it there. I'm giving you the chance to grab hold of life again.' She gave a little shrug. 'I'm not saying it's going to be easy. But it's surely worth a try. At least, if you're busy, you won't have time to brood.'

Janene had been listening, dull-eyed, but now she summoned up a smile and said with affection, 'Sally, you're a wonderful friend. No one could ask for any better. But there's really no need to worry about me. The fact is that I'm getting married shortly.'

Sally's eyes widened and her mouth opened in astonishment. 'Janene! That's marvellous!' She leaned across the table in excitement. 'You've got to tell me all about him. I'll bet he's absolutely gorgeous. What's his name? Is he rich? Not that that matters, but it helps. Where did you meet him?'

She laughed. 'Hold on! One thing at a time. First of all, his name is Damien. He's tall, with brown hair and grey eyes. He works for himself. He's a financial adviser and I met him six months ago.'

'Six months ago! And you've been keeping him to yourself all this time! Why didn't you let me know?'

'I—I was getting around to it,' she murmured. 'Anyway, I want you to be my bridesmaid at the wedding. Will you?'

'Just try and stop me,' Sally threatened, bubbling over with enthusiasm. 'When is the wedding?'

'Well, we haven't actually got round to fixing the

date yet,' Janene confessed quietly. 'Damien is very busy at the moment.'

Sally's eyebrows rose a fraction. 'I see. . . You mean, he's going to marry you when he can spare the time?' Giving her head a slight shake of disapproval, she took another sip of her coffee, then laid her cup down and sighed in apology. 'I'm sorry. I shouldn't have said that. At least he sounds as if he'll be a good provider.' She smiled brightly. 'So? When am I going to meet him? Just let me know the time and place. I'll dust off one of my old boyfriends and we'll have a foursome. Dinner, then a nightclub.'

The idea appealed to Janene. 'I'd like that, Sally. I really would like you to meet him. I'll be out of town for a few days, but as soon as I get back I'll get in touch and let you. . .' Her voice trailed off and the colour drained from her face as she caught sight of the man at the bar.

Sally eyed her with concern. 'What's wrong? Do you feel ill?'

The man had his back to them, but he was tall and slim and had raven-black hair and a way of standing. . . He turned to greet a companion and Janene let out a sigh of relief. 'It—it's nothing,' she stammered. 'I thought I saw someone I met at a party last night.'

Sally turned in her seat. 'Do you mean that dishy-looking guy at the bar?'

'Yes. But I was wrong.' This was ridiculous, she told herself. She was acting like a nervous idiot. The chances of her ever running into Kassim Riffik again were negligible. He was probably back in Morocco by now, where he belonged.

'So, what did this man at the party do to scare you?'

asked Sally, eager for a bit of gossip. 'And don't say
that he didn't. You looked as if you'd seen a ghost a
moment ago.'

'Nothing,' she answered firmly. 'It was all in my
imagination.' Before Sally could interrogate her any
further on the subject, she called the waiter over and
settled the bill with her credit card. 'It's my treat,' she
announced to Sally. 'And don't argue.'

The first boutique they'd opened, The Cat's Eye, was
only a few minutes' walk away and Sally insisted on
dragging her along to see her latest range of stock. The
manageress took the opportunity for a break, and as
Janene took her place behind the glass-topped counter
she felt a stirring of familiar excitement.

She was busy casting a professional eye over the
display when a customer came in, and it seemed the
most natural thing in the world to switch on her sales
technique. Ten minutes later the woman, who'd only
come in for a pair of ear-rings, happily left with a
matching bracelet and necklace.

'You haven't lost the touch,' Sally remarked in
approval. 'And you were really enjoying yourself. Go
on. . .admit it. You feel at home behind that counter,
don't you?'

Janene looked around the boutique regretfully, then
shook her head. 'My mind is made up, Sally. I'm getting
married.'

'Yes——' Sally gave a despondent shrug '—so you've
told me. But if things don't work out. . . Well, you
know where to come.'

It was just after five in the evening when Janene arrived
at the cottage in the depths of the Kent countryside.

On the way she'd stopped at the supermarket in Ashford and loaded up the Volvo with enough tinned and frozen food to last a fortnight.

Isolated and hidden behind high hedges, the cottage was half timbered, with a thatched roof and strong shutters on the windows. An ideal retreat from the world. It had belonged to her parents, and she'd spent many happy weekends here as a child.

A few weeks after her parents' funeral she'd come down, intending to spend some time on her own, but the memories it evoked were too painful and she'd fled back to London after only one night. For a while after that she'd toyed with the idea of selling the cottage, but then she'd met Damien and he'd persuaded her to change her mind. The cottage was a sound investment, he'd said, and though the market for this type of property was depressed at the moment it was bound to pick up sooner or later.

The place smelt damp and musty after being closed up for so long, but she soon had a log fire blazing in the hearth, then, arming herself with a bottle of red wine and a glass, she went into the kitchen and began preparing a light supper. The memories weren't so bad now. She was learning to live with them.

The following day was warm and sunny and, throwing the windows and doors wide open, she vacuumed and scrubbed and polished the place from top to bottom. By evening she was stiff and aching, but everything was done to her satisfaction, and she rewarded herself with a long, luxuriating soak in the bath.

That night, relaxing with a glass of wine in front of another blazing fire, she was glad that she'd taken Damien's advice to hold on to the cottage. Instead of selling it, she'd keep it. When they were married, this would be the ideal place to relax and unwind. The nearest house was half a mile away, so there were no noisy neighbours to disturb the peace and tranquillity. And eventually, of course, they'd be able to bring their own children here. Her parents would have liked that if they'd still been alive.

A sudden noise from outside caught her attention and drew her to the window. She peered out into the night but saw nothing. It had sounded like a rattle from the gate at the foot of the path, and she opened the door and called out nervously, 'Who's there? What do you want?'

There was no answer from the menacing darkness, and she strained her ears. From the woods to the left there was a fluttering of wings and the hoot of an owl. The river at the back of the cottage gurgled softly.

She stood for a moment longer, her breath quick and nervous, then, biting her lip, she closed the door and made sure that it was securely locked and bolted.

Pouring herself another glass of wine, she sat down by the fire again and told herself not to be such a coward. It had probably been nothing more sinister than a fox out foraging for scraps. It was that man Riffik who was to blame for the state of her nerves. All that talk about corsairs snatching people from their beds. Well, there was little chance of an ocean-going boat making its way up that little river.

No, she decided. She had nothing to fear from him. Damien had been right. Kassim Riffik was the hot-blooded Mediterranean type. All talk and come-to-bed eyes. Chatting up strange women was just a way of life to men like him, as natural as eating and drinking.

Her thoughts turned to Damien. She was going to have to be firm and get him to agree to a date for the wedding. When she'd had to make that ridiculous excuse to Sally about him being too busy at the moment, she'd felt embarrassed. After all, it only took half an hour at the most to get married in a register office. If he could afford to take a week's holiday and come down here, he could surely afford the time off for a half-hour ceremony.

The heat of the fire and the wine she'd drunk were making her drowsy. The sensible thing to do was to go to bed, but she was too comfortable sitting right here, and slowly her eyelids began to droop. Her last thought before she fell asleep was that she'd have to check all the window-latches before she retired for the night. . .

The fire was low, although the room was still warm, when she opened her eyes. There was a strange prickling sensation in her arm, but she ignored it as she stared up at the dark stranger who was bending over her.

'Hello, Janene. How are you feeling?'

His features were slightly blurred, but there was no mistaking those blue eyes. 'I knew I was going to dream about you,' she mumbled. She felt as if she was floating on a warm, spongy cloud.

'Yes. I said we'd meet again, didn't I?'

'I know you did. That's why I'm dreaming about you.' She was pleased at how clever she was to have worked that out.

'Can you stand?' he asked quietly.

'Of course I can stand,' she said indignantly. She

struggled to her feet and swayed. Peering into his face, she said, 'There! I'm standing.'

'Hmm. . .' He shook his head doubtfully. 'I think I'd better carry you.'

She smiled. 'Go ahead.' He lifted her easily and, as he cradled her in his arms, she clasped her hands around his neck. 'I suppose you're going to take me through to the bedroom now.' His lips were enticingly close and she felt reckless and abandoned. After all, this was her dream and she could do anything she damn well pleased.

'Do you want me to take you to bed?' he asked softly.

'I don't mind,' she replied, her eyes fixed firmly on his mouth. 'After all those things you said to me at the party, it might be interesting to find out if you're as good as you think you are.'

He gave a deep, throaty chuckle. 'I am. But we don't have time at the moment. That pleasure will have to wait till later.'

She frowned. This dream was getting disappointing. 'Later might be too late,' she said grumpily. 'I could wake up at any minute.'

'And if you did happen to wake up, you'd undoubtedly slap my face and demand to be put down immediately?' he asked with a touch of irony.

She thought that over for a moment, then nodded. 'Yes. I'd have to, wouldn't I? I mean. . .I'm getting married to Damien very soon. I'd be cheating on him.' His mouth was still close to hers and she wanted desperately to feel it against her own. Then slowly the dream began to fade, and she descended into a warm cocoon of darkness.

\* \* \*

Someone was shaking her shoulder gently and she murmured sleepily, 'Go away. I'm tired.'

The shaking persisted, and a woman's voice with a French accent said, 'We will be landing soon. I have brought you some tea. Drink it and you'll feel better.'

Janene cautiously opened her eyes and took in her surroundings. Another dream. She was in a tiny lounge. . .sitting in a comfortable seat. The windows were small and she looked out. Well! This was a new twist! She'd never dreamt of being in a plane before.

'Please. . .take your tea.'

The girl was smiling at her. A pretty little stewardess in a light grey uniform. A door at the front of the lounge opened and Kassim entered. He took the cup from the stewardess and waited until she had departed back to the galley, then he said matter-of-factly, 'This is mint tea. It's very refreshing. I'm sure you'll like it.'

Her eyes grew wider and the first stirrings of panic rose in her throat. This wasn't a dream! This was real! She could even smell the mint in the tea from here. Looking at him in utter disbelief, she spluttered, 'You—you've kidnapped me!'

A hint of mockery glinted from his blue eyes. 'Yes. . .I suppose it appears that way to you.' He offered her the cup once more. 'Do you want this or not?'

'You've kidnapped me!' she repeated in a voice of incredulity. 'You came to the cottage last night! I—I thought I was dreaming.'

'That would be the effect of the drug,' he said calmly. 'But you've no need to——'

'You drugged me?' She shot to her feet in outrage and dashed the cup from his hand.

He surveyed the broken china and stained carpet at his feet, and shook his head. 'Tut, tut. I didn't realise that English girls went in for smashing crockery. I thought it was only volatile Italian ladies who did things like that.' He looked up and gave her an apologetic shrug. 'I merely administered a sedative which——'

'You stuck a damned needle in my arm,' she accused him hotly. 'I remember feeling it now.'

He went on smoothly, 'As I was saying, a sedative which is perfectly safe and non-addictive. It's the same thing they give to patients in hospital a few hours before an operation. It soothes and calms the nerves.'

'So now you're a doctor, are you?' she fumed.

'I studied medicine in Paris for five years,' he informed her casually, then added, 'Anyway, it was imperative that I got you to safety before the police arrived.' He smiled at her look of incredulity and explained, 'I was informed at the very last minute by certain. . .friends of mine that officers from the Drug Squad were due to swoop on the cottage at five a.m.'

She snorted. 'Well, if that's the best you can come up with——'

'Damien dealt in cocaine,' he informed her quietly. 'A lot of the stuff is cached somewhere in your cottage.'

She stared at him in angry silence for a moment, then snapped, 'I've never heard such rubbish in my life. I don't believe a word of it. You're making it up.'

'And that's precisely why I had to sedate you,' he pointed out. 'There was no time to argue with you, or to search the cottage and get rid of the stuff before the police arrived.' He paused, then went on reflectively, 'I've no doubt that you'd have been able to prove your innocence eventually, but you might have had to spend a few uncomfortable weeks in custody. I sincerely regret having had to resort to such tactics, but I had no alternative.'

'Oh, you're going to regret it all right!' she promised heatedly. 'Assault and kidnapping and—and slanderous accusations against an innocent man. As soon as we land I'm going to report you to the authorities. You'll probably spend the rest of your life in prison.'

His eyes were unwavering, and his thin lips stretched and twisted into a cynical smile. 'I'm sorry to dash your hopes for my downfall. When we arrive at our destination, you'll find that I'm the only authority there is.' He paused and studied her expression, then added drily, 'However, if you submit your complaints to me in writing I'll attend to them in due course.'

She sat down in defeat and glared up at him. It was a long time since she'd felt as outraged as this. Things like this weren't supposed to happen in this day and age. At least, not in England. My God, you weren't even safe in your own house at night! Suddenly she lurched to her feet again and strode towards the lounge door.

His arm shot out and restrained her. 'Where do you think you're going?'

'To see the pilot,' she snapped, struggling to get past. 'I'm going to tell him what's happened and demand that he turn back and take me home immediately.'

His dark face hovered over hers and he teased softly, 'How beautiful you look when you're in a temper. There's a glow on your skin and a positive sparkle in your eyes.'

'Let me pass!' she demanded furiously.

He lowered his arm and shrugged. 'Go ahead. But

you'll be wasting your time. This is my plane and the pilot only obeys my orders.'

She drew in her breath. 'Your plane?'

He flashed his white teeth at her in a smile of affirmation, then said, 'Perhaps you'd like to sit down now and I'll have "my" stewardess fetch you another drink.'

She slumped down in her seat and looked up at him bleakly. She was beginning to remember, with some embarrassment, the things she'd said to him last night in her dream-state, before the sedative had taken full effect.

'What happened after I passed out last night?' she asked suspiciously.

He pressed a bell for the stewardess, ordered another cup of tea, then drawled, 'After you passed out I carried you outside, put you in a car, drove you to a private airfield and lifted you aboard this plane.'

'And that's all that happened?' she asked doubtfully.

His blue eyes narrowed and became icy. 'I hope you're not suggesting that I took advantage of your condition?'

'Why not?' she retorted. 'You've done everything else. I wouldn't put it past you.' She stared back at him resentfully. 'You say that you studied medicine and that you own this plane. That means you're a man of intelligence, at least. If that's the case, can you tell me why you're doing a stupid thing like this? I've got a good idea what you've got in mind, but it won't do you any good.'

He raised a mocking eyebrow. 'Don't be too sure. I recall the conversation we had at the party. You told me that you had nothing against me as a person and that, in fact, you found me quite attractive.'

Her mouth dropped open in protest, then she reminded him acidly, 'I also called you egotistical. That was the understatement of the year, now I come to think about it. A dangerous and conceited oaf would have been nearer the mark.'

'My faults are many,' he conceded with a crooked grin. 'But in time you will learn to overlook them. After those amorous overtures you made to me last night, I have every confidence in our future relationship. You and I, Janene, are going to give each other exquisite and eternal pleasure.'

His reference to last night made her inwardly cringe, but she said coldly, 'So it doesn't mean anything to you that I'm in love with another man?'

His deep laugh grated across her raw, exposed nerves. 'You may have intended to marry Damien, but I doubt if you were ever seriously in love with him.'

She felt herself flushing, and was on the point of retaliating with some crushing remark when the stewardess returned and handed her a fresh cup.

Conscious of Kassim's blue eyes stripping and caressing her in anticipation, she sipped the tea, then laid down the cup and averted her head to stare out of the window. Far below, she saw green rollers and white surf washing along countless miles of deserted golden beach. Inland there was nothing but scrub growing in a barren landscape of red earth and rock.

'Would you mind telling me where we are?' she asked bitterly.

He chuckled. 'The far side of the moon,' he said, reminding her of the sarcastic statement she'd made at the party. Satisfied that he'd scored a point, he went on, 'What you see below you is the Atlantic Ocean and the coast of south-west Morocco.'

She simmered away in silence for a few more minutes as he settled himself in the seat beside her. Dark, suspicious thoughts were tormenting her mind and the more she tried to ignore them the more persistent they became. Undoubtedly she'd get to the truth sooner or later, but her more immediate problem was how to deal with this situation.

Her nerves tautened and her leg twitched as he placed his hand on her thigh, just above the knee. 'Don't be discouraged by the view, Janene,' he whispered in a voice of silky seduction. 'I'm offering you much more than rocks and sand. You will shortly find yourself in a private little corner of paradise.'

His hand began gently stroking her thigh, but, instead of telling him to stop, she said unsteadily, 'I—I don't care what it's like. You—you can't keep me there against my will.'

'I won't need to,' he murmured in her ear. 'Once you have drunk at my well, no water will ever taste as sweet again. You will stay because you will be a prisoner of your own awakened desires.'

Her chest was getting tight, and she gulped, 'Are all Moroccan men as conceited as you are? If they are, then I pity the poor women who have to put up with it.'

'Not conceited, my little English rose. Just confident in the knowledge that we are experts in the art of physical pleasure. In our culture, it's a man's duty to recognise and cater for a woman's needs.' He gave her thigh a final squeeze, then said, with tongue in cheek, 'There is nothing I would like better than to give you a demonstration here and now, I myself have a desire that needs urgent consummation, but my appetite shall remain under control for the moment.' His hand came up and slid sensuously across her stomach, causing her heart to race. He reached for her seatbelt, and gave her a wide and wicked smile. 'We'll be landing shortly. Allow me to strap you in.'

# CHAPTER THREE

THE plane was banking gently to the left, giving her a good view of the scene below. Atop a craggy headland that thrust its way out into the sea in defiance of the crashing rollers were the ruins of an ancient fort. This crumbling reminder of a dark and violent past overlooked a busy harbour which was filled with colourful fishing-boats. Behind the ruins lay the town, a sprawling, disorganised jumble of square white buildings and narrow, twisting alleyways. Beyond the town, terraced riverbanks were green with fruit and palm-trees, while down at the river-edge women pounded their washing on stones.

The 'airport' was nothing more than a cleared strip of scrubland about two miles east of the town. In a cloud of dust the plane touched down and rolled to a halt in front of a huge, barn-like shed.

Kassim undid his seatbelt, then helped her to her feet. The stewardess opened the door, and as Janene looked out she saw the heatwaves shimmering in the air.

The driver of a stretched limousine already had the rear door opened and, as soon as she and Kassim were settled in the air-conditioned interior, he sped towards the town.

Acutely conscious of her helpless situation, she sat in prim, tight-lipped silence. Perhaps the way to deal with him was to treat him with total indifference, to retreat into a world in which he played no part. The ultimate snub. No one could put up with that for long. Least of all a man with an ego as big as his.

Then again, she wondered uneasily, was it really possible to ignore a man whose eyes could strip you at a glance and whose slightest touch sent flames of desire rampaging through your body? Well, she'd never been put to the test yet, but she knew she was going to find out before long.

The car approached the town in a swirl of red dust, and slowed down as its progress was hampered by the other traffic making its way into town: tall, robed men leading camels, or donkeys laden with baskets, or small herds of sheep and goats. Soon the streets became narrower and more crowded until, within the town centre proper, the pace was reduced to a mere crawl as the car inched and snaked its way through the crowded alleyways.

Even with the car windows closed, she could hear the bedlam of noise. Above the tinny blare of hundreds of transistor radios, merchants cried their wares and customers haggled over prices. Women, laden with baskets, babies clinging to their backs, drew their robes tighter and pushed their way through the jostling mass of humanity.

Beyond the market-place the road widened and, directly ahead of her, overlooking the squat, whitewashed houses, Janene could see the ruined fort. Suddenly the driver made a sharp left-hand turn and drew up outside a massive, iron-studded door set in a stone archway. At a blast from the horn the door swung inwards and the car entered a large courtyard.

At Kassim's prompting, she reluctantly got out and

studied her surroundings in silence. The walls were high, and as she heard the servants close and bolt the heavy door she bit her lip. The feeling of being trapped and at this man's mercy tightened a knot in her stomach.

Taking her firmly by the arm, Kassim led her past an ornamental fountain and colourful flowerbeds towards another door. With a display of gallantry, he opened it and ushered her through into an inner courtyard and, despite her resolution to maintain an air of indifference, her eyes widened and she stifled a gasp. The surrounding walls were covered in decorative tiles, while masses of flowers made a glorious blaze of colour: datura, dahlias, sunflowers, oleanders, and geraniums in tall, clay pots. Right at the centre there was a sunken swimming-pool in sea-green marble. At the far side of the courtyard an archway led to the interior of the house. She took a quick glance around, impressed by its elegance and décor—priceless carpets on the floor and solid mahogany, French-style furniture. In the air hung the sweet smell of cedarwood.

Kassim peeled off his jacket and tossed it carelessly aside. 'This is the end of our journey, Janene. Do you think you'll be comfortable here?'

She tried her best to ignore him, but was finally forced by his insistent stare to offer a nonchalant shrug.

His eyes glittered with amusement. 'Too overcome with awe to find your tongue?' he asked solicitously. 'Ah, well, that's understandable. *C'est magnifique, n'est-ce pas?*'

It certainly was, she thought darkly, but he'd probably stolen it.

He took her by the arm again. 'Come along and I'll show you the rest of the place.'

A marble stairway led to the upper part of the house. Throwing open a door, he invited her inside. It was cool and dark until he opened the shutters on the window overlooking the pool in the courtyard below.

'This will be our bedroom,' he announced cheerfully.

'What the hell do you mean, "our" bedroom?' she demanded fiercely, her vow of silence shattered.

'What's wrong? Isn't the bed large enough?' he enquired, with a mocking lift of his dark eyebrows. He eyed the bed doubtfully. 'You may be right. In the throes of passion we may end up on the floor. I'll have it changed immediately.'

'I'm not sleeping anywhere with you,' she said hotly. 'If I have to be incarcerated in this Hollywood film-set, I demand a room of my own.'

His blue eyes taunted her. 'I'm sure I can persuade you to change your mind. Just think of all the fun you'll be missing.'

She folded her arms, tapped her foot and glared at him.

'Hmm. . .' he drawled. 'Your skin has gone that wonderful colour again. Is it only your face that's affected, or does that flush spread over your entire body? I must satisfy my curiosity.' He raised his hand and beckoned her closer with his finger. 'Come here, my little English rose.'

'Stop calling me that,' she grated. 'I'm not your little anything.'

He derided her with a sardonic smile. 'There's no sense in postponing the inevitable. You're only making things awkward.'

'Good!' she snapped. 'I intend to be as awkward as I can until you stop all this nonsense and let me go home.'

He spread his arms and looked surprised. 'But this is your home from now on. What do you have in England to compare with luxury and comfort such as this?'

'Control of my own life, for one thing,' she retorted. 'Freedom of choice and freedom to go where I like.' She paused, then added bitterly, 'And the right not to be dictated to by anyone.'

'Control of one's own life is an illusion,' he replied smoothly. 'We are all the victims of fate and circumstance. One can only make the best of what one is given.'

She gave a sigh of exasperation. 'I'm not interested in entering into a philosophical debate with you.'

'Good,' he drawled. 'Women shouldn't concern themselves over such matters. As for freedom. . .you can leave the house any time you like. I shall provide a suitable escort for you. You can go into the town or down to the beach.'

'And my escort will make sure I go no further?' she asked drily.

'You would get lost in the desert,' he pointed out in a tone of dire warning. 'If you were lucky, you would die of thirst. If you were unlucky, you would be caught by some tribe of wandering outcasts who'd make you wish that you had died of thirst.' He appealed to her with a fiendish smile that made her think of a shark getting ready for lunch. 'On the other hand, if you stay here you will be given anything your heart desires. Within reason, of course.'

The resentment in her green eyes turned to resigned

acceptance. 'All right. . .' she said in a dull voice. 'Is it within reason to ask for something to eat? I've had nothing since supper last night.'

He looked contrite, but it was probably just an act. The only thing he seemed to take seriously was his avowed intention of getting her into bed.

'A thousand pardons,' he intoned. 'I am remiss in my duties as a host.' He strode over to the wall and pressed a button to summon a servant, then grinned at her, 'What would you like to order, Janene? A plate of figs? Some almonds? Goat-cheese?'

'No, thanks,' she said grimly. 'I'd like orange juice, coffee, toast and marmalade and two soft-boiled eggs.'

He gave an ironic little smile. 'A typical English breakfast. You'd rather cling to familiar customs than face the unknown?'

'I've had goat-cheese and I don't like it,' she informed him coldly. 'And I'll also need fresh clothes. You didn't give me the opportunity to pack before you drugged me.'

'Clothes will be provided,' he assured her smoothly.

'I don't mean those funny black robes I saw the women in town wearing,' she warned. 'Jeans will do fine.'

'Determined not to go native?' he asked mockingly. 'A pity. I think a caftan or *haik* would suit you.'

She was about to tell him that the native clothes she'd seen so far were the drabbest she'd ever encountered, when she caught sight of the young girl gliding silently into the room. Slim, with large, dark, liquid eyes, she was dressed in a robe of shimmering turquoise with gold edging. A headscarf of the same material was drawn under her chin and tied on top.

She smiled shyly at Janene and bowed to Kassim.

For a while he stood talking to her in some strange, guttural tongue, then she bowed again and drifted out of the room, as silent as a falling leaf.

'Well, Janene, breakfast will be served by the poolside in half an hour,' he informed her briskly. He pointed to the door. 'You can shower and freshen up there, meanwhile. Kebira will fetch you something suitable to wear.'

'Kebira?'

'The servant-girl you just saw. From now on she is your personal maid.'

She looked at him in surprise, then said firmly, 'I don't want a personal maid. I'm quite capable of looking after myself.'

'Are you really?' he asked with cynical amusement. 'That isn't the impression you've given me up till now. When you're left to your own devices you seem to get yourself into all kinds of trouble.' He saw the red spots of anger on her cheeks, and went on in a placating tone, 'Come, now, Janene. It isn't much to ask. As my consort, it's only fitting that you should have a personal maid. Besides, Kebira will feel terribly insulted and depressed if you reject her. In her eyes, it is a great honour to be chosen for such an important position in the household.'

She rolled her eyes heavenwards, then said scathingly, 'Kidnapping and emotional blackmail. There's nothing you'll stop at to get your way, is there?'

He shrugged. 'A talent I inherited from my illustrious ancestors. Now, I suggest that we bathe together and enjoy the pleasure of——'

'I'll bathe by myself,' she cut in icily. 'You can go and cool off in the swimming-pool.'

He heaved a sigh of disappointment, then gave a philosophical shrug. 'No matter. I can wait. The greater the hunger, the more satisfying the meal.' His blue eyes taunted her mercilessly, then they hardened. 'It would be inadvisable to try my patience too long, however. I'm a man who doesn't take kindly to being thwarted in his ambitions. That is another trait I inherited from my ancestors.'

As he strode from the room his threat still rang in her ears, making her skin prickle, and she hurriedly locked herself in the bathroom.

Everything she'd seen about this house so far spoke of pampered luxury, and the bathroom was no exception. There was a sunken bath in coral-pink marble, large enough to keep a school of dolphins happy, and, unless she was mistaken, the taps were solid gold. The walls and ceiling were covered in dazzling ceramic tiles, as were the two shower-stalls. An adjoining room held a sauna and an exercise area with more equipment than would be found in the average gym. Behind a partition she found dozens of coloured bath-towels and robes. There was even a selection of shower-caps, and, grabbing what she needed, she made her way to one of the showers and began undressing.

As soon as the water ran hot she stepped under the shower and closed her eyes in relaxation. After a few moments she began lazily soaping herself, and her thoughts turned to Kassim. Disturbing yet exciting thoughts. In her imagination he was here beside her, his dark and lithe body naked and glistening. As they moved over her breasts, her hands became his hands.

She threw her head back and her body became taut and receptive to the waves of sensual pleasure sweeping——

Suddenly her mind snapped into place, and, angry at her weakness and lack of self-control, she turned the shower off. Dammit! She was the one who should have been cooling off in the pool.

Kebira was waiting patiently in the bedroom with a selection of underwear and clothes spread out on the bed. She immediately smiled and began chattering away excitedly.

Janene returned the smile and raised a restraining hand. 'Hold on, Kebira! Can't you speak English?'

The large, liquid eyes blinked solemnly.

'*Français?*'

Another blink. '*Oui, madame. Un—un peu.*'

'Never mind. I only speak it *un peu* myself. We'll get along fine in sign-language.' She looked at the display on the bed and wondered where all the brand-new underwear had come from. His harem's wardrobe-mistress, probably. The underwear was mostly silk, and there were fabulously coloured robes and caftans, blouses and skirts. But not a pair of jeans in sight.

She eventually settled for black silk trousers and a white silk blouse. The trousers were loose and baggy and tied at the ankles, and the blouse was covered in exotic embroidery.

When she had completed her dressing, she examined herself critically in front of a large mirror until Kebira dragged her by the hand, made her sit at a dressing-table, then attacked the mass of red hair with a silver-backed hairbrush.

Kassim was at a table by the poolside when she went

down. Rising gallantly to his feet, he eyed her with approval as she approached, and greeted her with a flash of white teeth and an elaborate bow. 'Never has my pitiful abode been graced by such beauty. The flowers weep with envy.'

He was wearing a blue, white-lined belted tunic over his shirt and he seemed taller, darker, and more strikingly handsome than ever.

The table was already set, and as he poured her coffee he said affably, 'My miserable wretch of a cook is at this very moment trembling in his shoes. I have ordered him to be flogged if everything is not to your satisfaction.'

She eyed him warily across the table. He was joking, of course. She sincerely hoped so, but he was such an enigmatic character that one could never tell. They both ate in silence. The coffee was perfect, but the eggs were hard-boiled. Not that she would even have contemplated the idea of complaining, however. His breakfast seemed to consist entirely of fruit—orange segments and dates—which he ate without once taking his eyes from her.

'You're very quiet, Janene,' he observed at last. 'Something on your mind?' he asked innocently.

Looking directly into his clear blue eyes, she said bitterly, 'I've got plenty on my mind. You, most of all. And Damien, for another.'

The smile on his face became a little bleak and he growled, 'It's time you forgot all about your precious Damien.'

'Really?' She sipped her coffee. 'And how do I do that? Just pretend that he never existed?'

'That's as good a way as any,' he agreed drily. 'And you can start by removing that ring from your finger.'

She hastily put her left hand in her lap and scowled at him. 'I don't know how you did it, but you must have tricked Damien somehow.'

'Did I?' he taunted.

'It's the only thing that makes sense,' she muttered. 'Damien was the only person who knew I'd be at the cottage last night. So somehow you tricked him into telling you where to find me.'

She waited for some kind of denial, but all he offered her was a smile of bland indifference. Very well. . .that meant that her accusation was true. The only question remaining now was why. No man would go to all the trouble he'd taken, just to get a woman into bed. A fool with an obsession might, but Kassim was no fool.

'You'll find out all in good time,' he drawled when she put it to him.

'I want to know now,' she demanded furiously.

He chewed reflectively on a date, then shook his head. 'No, Janene. It would only upset you.'

Her green eyes widened in astonishment. 'I can't be any more upset than you've already made me,' she fumed. She glared at him for a moment, then snapped, 'Perhaps Damien beat you in some business deal and you decided to get your revenge by stealing his girl.'

He gave a sigh of impatience. 'It's much more complicated than that. Now, can we talk about something else? The subject of your ex-fiancé bores me.'

'Well, it doesn't bore me,' she persisted vehemently, banging her cup back into the saucer. 'I want to know! Here and now! I demand to——' Her voice skidded to an embarrassed halt as she saw with horror that the handle of the delicate, probably priceless cup had broken off and was still looped around her forefinger. Dry-mouthed, she tried to stammer an apology, then saw him rise to his feet and stalk round the table towards her.

She looked up at him helplessly. 'I—I'm sorry. I didn't mean to. . .'

Gently he removed the remains of the handle from her finger and frowned. 'Are you cut?'

He was bending down, his dark face uncomfortably close to hers, and she said weakly, 'No. It—it seems all right.'

His face inched nearer. 'Good. That's all that matters.' Now their lips were almost touching and her heart began to pound. 'Cups can be replaced,' he murmured softly. 'Don't worry about it. I'll send out for a few hundred more. That should keep you going until you learn to control that fiery temper.'

'I—I haven't. . .got a—a temper,' she protested, in a strangled whisper that died in a whimper as his lips closed over hers. The touch was gentle at first, nothing more than a warm tingle, and she caught the scent of him—very male, fresh and spice-laden. Gradually he increased the pressure, his lips teasing and nibbling over hers with a sensual friction that sent delicious little tremors to the soles of her feet. Then her heart thudded and sang in her ears as she felt his tongue probing, testing her defences and demanding entry. Her mouth opened like a flower in the heat of his onslaught. This was wrong! This was dangerous! But the faint, warning voice of her conscience went unheeded in the waves of feverish passion engulfing her very soul. One of his hands was on the back of her chair, the other on the table, while her own lay helplessly in her lap. The only contact between them was their mouths, and that lent a feeling of deliberate, erotic dalliance that served to heighten her sensual pleasure. His tongue continued to explore the warm sweetness of her mouth and she responded with hungry enthusiasm. Something in the depths of her mind was wringing its hands in despair at her shocking behaviour, but something else, a little more wicked, told it to mind its own damn business and banged the door shut.

Suddenly his mouth withdrew from hers, leaving her shaken and breathless, and he purred like a satisfied tiger. 'The sweetest hors-d'oeuvre I've ever had. Tonight we will enjoy the main course, Janene. A feast of love and sensuous pleasure such as you have never experienced.'

She raised her hands in a half-hearted attempt to push him away, but he caught her wrist in a grip of steel and smiled thinly. 'Already the blood is singing in your veins and your eyes are hot with desire. That one kiss has given you a tiny glimpse through the very gates of paradise and you hunger for more. Admit it, my sweet rose.'

Not on your life, she thought nervously. If she did give voice to her feelings, he was likely to throw her to the ground and prove how good he was, regardless of how many servants were peeping through the shutters. On the other hand, if she lied about it he might start kissing her again with increased fervour. If he started doing that again she'd be in danger of losing her self-respect.

How could any woman remain unyielding against such devastating sexual aggression? He was the prince of darkness and Genghis Khan rolled into one. Even now she could feel herself drowning in those blue eyes. . .being hypnotised. . .drawn under his spell.

'Look,' she said in desperation. 'Don't you have something else to do? Feed the camels or something? I—I'd like to be alone for a while.'

He released her wrist and straightened up with a grin. 'You've gone that delicate shade of pink again. But I'll bow to your wishes for the moment. I must give you time to gather your scattered wits. Just sit and relax for a while, and gloat over your good fortune at being here, while I attend to the mundane affairs of business. Meanwhile, if there is anything you should require, you merely have to signal to one of the servants and——' He paused and stiffened at the sudden commotion and noise from the outer courtyard. Suddenly the entrance to the inner courtyard swung open and a woman dashed through.

She was dressed in a shabby black robe and headscarf and couldn't have been much more than eighteen. At the sight of Kassim she rushed towards him and threw herself at his feet. Her hands scrabbled for the bottom of his cloak and she raised it and pressed it to her lips before turning a tear-stained face up to him imploringly, then beseeching him in a torrent of Arabic.

Janene was shocked and touched by the girl's obvious distress, and she stared at Kassim in reproach. He'd probably used this poor creature, then discarded her. Now she was back, begging him for a job in the kitchen. It was either that or something equally horrendous.

Kassim spoke sharply to the girl and she got to her feet. Speaking quietly now, he began questioning her, listening attentively to her answers and occasionally nodding his head in understanding. Finally he signalled to one of the servants, who came over and escorted the girl into the house.

Janene looked at him questioningly but, before she could open her mouth, he smiled over her shoulder as a second visitor appeared in the courtyard.

# CHAPTER FOUR

THE woman was a slim and well-preserved fifty-year-old, with dark hair, going grey, and bright, lively eyes. She was wearing a khaki bush-jacket and trousers and a large-brimmed hat, and when she spoke Janene detected a touch of soft Irish brogue in the voice.

'I'm sorry, Kassim,' the woman said. 'Jalila came to me with her problem and I assured her that I'd come and see you tomorrow. It looks as if she got a little impatient and decided to take things into her own hands.'

Kassim nodded gravely. 'Her action was understandable. I've sent her to the kitchen. She'll be fed and given something decent to wear. As for her husband—that spawn of a flea-infested goat—I have given orders that he is to appear before me at three o'clock this afternoon.' He waved the matter aside for the present, and smiled. 'Sister Mary, I would like you to meet Miss Janene Peters, from England.' His blue eyes flickered a brief warning at Janene, then went on glibly, 'We met while I was in London and she insisted on coming back with me to visit our wonderful country.'

The fraudulent claim took Janene's breath away by its sheer brazenness, but before she could splutter an angry denial the older woman was chirping away excitedly, 'Now, isn't that nice! Janene? What a pretty name. My dear, you'll fall in love with Morocco, just as I did all those years ago. If you come up against any problems or if there's anything at all I can help you with, just pop along and see me at my office in town. We can have a nice long chat and——'

Kassim, who'd been looking at Sister Mary with genuine affection, suddenly broke in, 'Why don't you take Janene into town with you now and show her around? She's at a loose end at the moment and I'm sure she'd enjoy the experience.' He grinned at Janene, but the challenge to contradict him was plain in the slight narrowing of his eyes.

'Sure, and I'd be delighted to!' enthused the older woman.

The first thought that popped into Janene's head was that this was her chance to make her escape. If she told this woman the true circumstances of her presence here, and appealed for help, surely she wouldn't refuse. There was bound to be a British consul in some nearby town she could phone.

But would Sister Mary believe her? Probably not, otherwise Kassim wouldn't have suggested the idea in the first place. On the other hand, a talk with this woman might prove profitable, and a few discreet questions about Kassim would give her a better understanding of the man, and whether he was an out-and-out rogue or not.

Five minutes later she was sitting in the passenger seat of a battered old Jeep as Sister Mary drove carefully towards the town centre. When the road began to narrow, she parked the Jeep next to a wall and stopped the engine. As they got out they were immediately surrounded by a horde of ragged children, holding out their hands and crying, 'Madame Marie! *Bon bons*! *Chocolat*!'

She ruffled a few heads, then, delving into one of the large pockets of the bush-jacket, she produced a bag of sweets and began distributing them.

Finally they made their escape, and as Sister Mary led the way towards the souk she laughed. 'Sure, and I wish I hadn't started. I handed out some sweets I'd brought back from France a few years ago and the little tykes have been plaguing me like the devil ever since.'

'Why do they call you Sister?' Janene asked politely. 'You don't dress like a nun.'

'I used to be,' the older woman explained cheerfully. 'I left the order ten years ago but the title just seems to stick. I work for the government now. Social and Medical Department. I run the clinic in town.'

They were drawing nearer to the souk now, and the cries and shouts from the market-place were getting louder. On either side of the road were high walls, blank except for an occasional heavily-grilled window. Now and again Janene caught sight of a veiled face staring down from a flat rooftop.

'Who was that young girl who came to the house just now?' she asked conversationally. 'She seemed terribly upset about something.'

Sister Mary gave a sigh and shook her head. 'Yes. That was Jalila. She's just been repudiated by her husband. She came to me for help. I don't know why. There's nothing I can do about it. I told her I'd ask Kassim's advice. Anyway, I'll be interested in seeing how he deals with the matter.'

Janene looked at her in puzzlement. 'Repudiated? What does that mean?'

'It means that her husband has divorced her,' she

explained, then added angrily, 'That's his third wife in six years.'

Janene raised her eyebrows. 'You'd think he'd be tired of going to court by now.'

'Court?' Mary gave a bitter laugh. 'A man doesn't need to go to court in this country. If he wants to divorce his wife he only has to say three times, "I repudiate thee", and that's it, as far as she's concerned. He doesn't even have to say it—he can put it in writing, and there's nothing the woman can do about it. She hasn't any claim against him and the law won't help her.'

Janene was horrified. 'But that's absolutely scandalous! Are you telling me he can just throw her out of the house?'

Mary gave a helpless little shrug. 'In theory he's supposed to feed her for a few months, but more often than not he just forgets her.'

My God! thought Janene. If that was how they carried on in Morocco they could keep it, as far as she was concerned. Her mind rebelled against a society where women were denied even the basic right of justice. 'Why did he divorce her?' she asked suspiciously.

'The same reason he divorced his first two wives.' Mary said with a touch of irony in her voice. 'She's barren. She can't give him any children. And in this country a married man without children—sons especially—is an object of contempt and ridicule.' She saw the look of disbelief and dismay on Janene's face, and said hurriedly, 'Don't get the wrong idea, my dear. Sure, and all Moroccan men aren't like him. There are plenty of good, decent men, like the *caid*.'

'Who's the *caid*?' Janene asked, wondering if she'd ever understand this place or the customs.'

'The *caid* is a tribal chief. Kassim is the chief of his tribe so he's the head man of the town.'

It was obvious from her tone that she held Kassim in high esteem, and Janene said, 'You mean he's a sort of mayor?'

Mary chuckled. 'You could say that. But Kassim doesn't need to get voted into power. He comes from a family that's been very powerful in this part of the country since the mists of time. By all accounts they were a bloodthirsty lot of ruffians, who went in for piracy and kidnapping and all sorts of terrible things. Anyway, it made them filthy rich, but I often feel that Kassim feels obligated to atone for his ancestors by being so generous.'

That might be so, Janene told herself sourly, but he was still keeping alive one of the old family traditions, at least. Abduction. 'Is it true that he studied medicine in Paris?' she asked, wondering if he'd told the truth about it.

Mary bobbed her head. 'Certainly. Kassim is a qualified doctor. He was working for the United Nations in the Sudan when his father died and he had to return here and take up the reins.'

They were entering the heart of the souk now, and Janene stopped her questioning for the time being. But there was still a lot she wanted to know before she made up her mind about the man.

The market was a bedlam of colour and noise. Everyone seemed to know Mary, and she returned their greetings with a friendly smile for the women and a sweet for the children. Janene, being a stranger, drew a few polite but guarded smiles.

Most of the goods were laid out on blankets on the ground or arranged haphazardly on hastily set-up tables. Her eye was suddenly caught by a stall selling jewellery, and she stopped to examine the display.

'Professional interest,' she explained to Mary. 'I used to be in this line back in London.' She examined some beautifully engraved silver bracelets and an assortment of amber and shell necklaces, judging the quality. Each item was handmade, which meant that no two were ever exactly the same. She smiled at the stallholder, a young girl in the inevitable black robe and headscarf, then she turned to Mary. 'Ask her where she gets this stuff.'

'Sure, and I don't have to·ask,' Mary answered cheerfully. 'Her father and her brother have a little workshop nearby.'

They moved on to the next stall, which was showing a brilliant display of richly embroidered caftans and headscarves. These too, she discovered, were locally produced. It was just a pity that Sally wasn't here on a stock-buying expedition. She'd have been as happy as a cat in a creamery.

About an hour later, when they were sitting in the shade outside a café, drinking mint tea and eating tiny sweet cakes, she was wondering how to turn the conversation back to Kassim when Mary unwittingly saved her the trouble by saying with concern, 'I hope that Kassim takes time to relax now that he's home again. He works far too hard. He's forever jetting off to Madrid or Paris or Rome on business. Sometimes he comes back quite exhausted.'

Yes, Janene thought wryly. Seducing women in all the major capitals of Europe was bound to be exhausting, even if you did have your own plane. 'I'm not quite sure what kind of business Kassim is in,' she admitted archly. 'Apart from being the head of this town, that is. When we. . .met in London he didn't get around to mentioning it.'

Mary laughed. 'Well, I'm not quite sure where to begin. First, there's the fish. Mackerel and sardines. He owns a fleet of boats that catch them and he owns the plant where they're canned and sent for export. Then, there are the hotels he owns all around the Mediterranean. There's trucking. . .and fuel distribution. Oh. . .and he has a couple of stud-farms for horses. Everything is managed by various members of his family—uncles, cousins, brothers. But Kassim is a man who likes to keep his finger on the pulse. That's why he's away so often.' She paused, then said hesitantly, 'It's about time he found himself a wife and settled down. When I saw you this morning I thought. . . But then I saw the ring on your finger. It's an engagement-ring, isn't it?'

'Yes,' Janene admitted calmly. 'My fiancé lives in London and his name is Damien.' Now ask me what I'm doing here with Kassim if my fiancé is back home, she challenged silently.

Mary, apparently deciding that it was none of her business, finished her tea, got to her feet and smiled chirpily. 'I'd like to show you round the new clinic. Kassim built and paid for it and it's better equipped than anything they've got in the larger cities. We're all very proud of it.'

* * *

Mary drove her back to the house a few minutes before three. In the inner courtyard they found Kassim gently questioning Jalila about her failed marriage. The girl was now wrapped in a magnificent robe of cornflower-blue, and she lowered her eyes in embarrassment at the presence of another two women.

Kassim spoke to her sharply and she raised her head in a gesture of pride and defiance.

'That's better,' Kassim growled in French. 'Don't act as if you've done anything to be ashamed of. Hassan, your husband, is the guilty party in this affair. When he arrives I want you to look him straight in the eye.'

Mary eyed him apologetically and murmured, 'Perhaps it would be better if Janene and I went into the house.'

'No,' Kassim said grimly. 'The more women who are witnesses to this, the greater will be his humiliation.' He gestured to a servant to bring two more chairs, then he drew Janene aside and grinned. 'Knowing how talkative Sister Mary can be, I presume she's told you all about Jalila?'

'Yes,' she answered stiffly. 'And I told her exactly what I think of the way the law treats women here.'

His mouth curved ironically and his laser-blue eyes gleamed with humour. 'So, no doubt you'd never dream of marrying a Moroccan?'

'You can bet your life on that,' she muttered. 'I expect security from a husband. I wouldn't want to be cast aside on a whim.'

'That's strange,' he taunted her softly. 'People should marry for love. Yet you merely demand security. Don't you think you've got your priorities wrong, Janene?'

She lowered her eyes, more disturbed by his question

than she cared to admit. His relentless assault against her principles was wearing her down, causing her to rethink her motivation, and some of the truths she was finding out about herself were hard to face up to.

She was thankfully spared any more of his provocative remarks by the arrival of a servant from the outer courtyard, who whispered in his ear.

Kassim nodded, gave his instructions to the servant, then sat down, gesturing at Jalila to take the chair on his left while Janene and Mary sat at his right.

As Jalila's ex-husband came through the entrance he caught sight of his reception-committee; his steps faltered and the greasy smile slipped from his face. He was short and squat, wearing a loose black robe over an expensive suit. Thick lips and bulbous eyes over a hooked nose suggested shady deals in hotel rooms. Janene couldn't imagine what a young girl as pretty as Jalila had ever seen in a middle-aged gargoyle like him. Of course, if he was rich and she was from a poor family, who could say what pressure she'd been under?

Kassim remained seated, his lean frame hunched forward with his elbow on his knee and his chin in his fist, his blue eyes glittering icily at the visitor.

Hassan came to a halt before them, his gaze darting from one to the other, blinking in surprise at the sight of his ex-wife. He swallowed, then bowed and said hoarsely, '*Selaam alikum*, Caid.'

'For the benefit of my guests, we will conduct this hearing in English,' Kassim informed him coldly. 'I know that you are acquainted with the language.'

Hassan spread his hands and said uneasily, 'That is so, Caid. But men such as you and I should not discuss our business in front of women.'

'You are not here to discuss business,' Kassim snapped. 'You are here to give me your reasons for divorcing your wife.'

The bulbous eyes grew even wider, and he spluttered in indignation, 'With humble respect, Caid, that is my affair and no one else's.'

Kassim stared at him in threatening silence.

Hassan's face darkened in fury and he glared murderously at his ex-wife. 'My wife was barren, Caid,' he said thickly. 'She is incapable of bearing me any children. For two years I have been planting my seed in infertile ground.'

Kassim considered the statement, then said quietly, 'That is indeed unfortunate.'

Hassan nodded vigorously. 'A man needs daughters to care for him in his old age and sons to carry on his enterprises. Without children a man is nothing. Already I am losing respect in the town. They point their fingers at me and laugh.'

Kassim eyed him stonily, then murmured, 'It would seem that fate has indeed been unkind to you. Your first wife was also barren, was she not?'

'Yes, Caid.'

'And the second?'

Hassan shifted uneasily, and a thin film of sweat glistened on his upper lip. 'She too was unfruitful.'

Kassim straightened in his chair and frowned. 'So. . . three wives in a row, and all of them barren. It hardly seems possible.'

Hassan spread his hands in appeal and rolled his eyes mournfully. 'I think I must have had a curse put upon me, Caid. Perhaps by someone jealous of my success in business. It is the only explanation.'

Janene felt nothing but loathing for the man. And did people here really believe in curses? Probably. At least, neither Mary nor Kassim seemed to be surprised by the assertion.

'Tell me, Hassan,' Kassim asked in a deceptively mild voice, 'have you any idea where your first two wives are?'

The question startled the man, and he shrugged. 'I presume they went back to their families in disgrace, Caid.'

Kassim shook his head. 'Jalila tells me that your first wife is reduced to begging for food in the streets of Marrakesh. The other exists by selling her body to strangers in the alleyways of Rabat. Does their plight not touch your heart?'

Hassan shot another look at Jalila, then shrugged. 'If they choose to act in such a way, it is no concern of mine. They are worthless creatures and I was a fool to take them as wives in the first place.'

Janene noticed the way Kassim's right fist clenched, and she thought for a moment that he was going to hurl himself at the man and beat him to a pulp. To tell the truth, that was exactly what she felt like doing.

'Jalila also tells me that she has four older sisters,' Kassim continued drily. They are all happily married to good, caring husbands. Between them they have four healthy children.'

Hassan spread his hands in appeal once more. 'Then it proves how unfortunate I am, Caid. Five sisters and I end up with the only one who cannot conceive. I am truly cursed.'

'Yes. . .you may be right,' Kassim drawled. 'But a more likely explanation springs to mind. Something that has nothing to do with the jinnees or sorcery. Perhaps Allah, in his infinite wisdom and mercy to all mankind, has decided that one of you is enough. He may have denied you the right of reproduction.'

The insinuation brought a look of furious indignation to the Arab's face, and he pointed a shaking finger at Jalila. 'There is nothing wrong with my manhood, as she well knows.'

Kassim permitted himself a thin smile, then said caustically, 'No matter how many times a gun is fired, it is no use if the bullets are blanks. A simple medical test will determine the truth.'

Hassan's face paled, and he remonstrated heatedly, 'No! I will not submit to such a test. It is a humiliation.'

Kassim stared at him, his eyes glacial, then he nodded. 'That, of course, is your choice. No one can force you to be examined.'

The Arab relaxed, and Janene felt a sense of frustration that Kassim seemed to be letting him off the hook so easily. But a moment later she knew that she'd underestimated the man.

'You have a fleet of twelve fishing-boats in the harbour?'

Hassan bobbed his head. 'Yes, Caid. Excellent craft with fine crews.'

'Good,' said Kassim briskly. 'Now hear my judgement. You will give me nine of your boats. I will sell them, and the money obtained shall be divided equally between your three ex-wives. Wisely invested, it will provide them with a measure of comfort and security for the rest of their lives.'

Hassan stared at him in outraged disbelief. 'You are exceeding your authority, Caid. The law doesn't require me to——' He shut his mouth abruptly as Kassim stood up and towered over him like some dark, avenging genie.

'I know what the law requires, you misbegotten piece of offal,' he snarled. 'And I know what it doesn't require. It doesn't, for example, say that I or anyone else in this town has to supply your boats with fuel. Neither does it say that my processing and canning plants have to buy your catches.'

'But—but I protest,' whined Hassan.

'Protest as much as you like, you garbage-sniffing jackal, but pay heed to this. If you go against my wishes, I'll make sure that your precious boats are banned from every harbour in Morocco, Spain and the Mediterranean. They will remain at anchor until they are nothing more than rotting hulks.'

The Arab was sweating profusely now, and he had the horrified expression of a man staring into the jaws of disaster. Obviously he knew that Kassim had the power to carry out his threat. 'This—this isn't justice, Caid,' he stammered. 'Because I will not submit myself to—to this ridiculous medical test, you intend to ruin me.'

'It has nothing to do with your refusal to take the test,' Kassim growled. 'My decision was made before you came here.' He paused, and surveyed the Arab contemptuously. 'The Koran teaches us to be merciful, but you have shown little mercy towards the women you have used and cast aside. Now, to show that even I can be merciful, I will ask you once more to take the test. If the result is in your favour, you may keep six of your boats. But if it proves otherwise, then you will forfeit every one of them and you will be the one begging for bread in Marrakesh. The choice is yours. Make it now.'

The Arab's face was ashen and his voice was a mere strangled whisper. 'No test, Caid. I—I will give you nine of my boats.'

'Yes. . . I thought you would,' taunted Kassim. 'You are not quite so sure of your manly virility as you would have everyone believe.' He made an abrupt gesture of dismissal. 'My lawyer and accountant shall call on you tomorrow to make the arrangements. Now, remove yourself. Your foul presence has polluted my house long enough.'

Dinner was served promptly at eight. Kebira led Janene to the dining-room, then gave a little bow and withdrew, closing the doors behind her.

Kassim, busy at an ornate drinks cabinet, paused in the act of pouring two glasses of wine, turned, and surveyed her with open admiration. 'Magnificent!' he breathed. 'Breathtaking! A true vision of beauty!'

Kebira had thrown up her hands in despair at her mistress's idea of what constituted proper attire for dinner, and Janene, more to placate her maid than anything else, had allowed herself to be swathed in a robe of shimmering pale green silk, fastened at the shoulder by an enormous silver clip. On her feet she wore tiny yellow *babouches*—slippers—but she'd drawn the line at wearing the ubiquitous headscarf.

As Kassim handed her the glass she took in the splendour of the table, set with candles, gleaming silver and china spread over a snowy damask tablecloth.

A servant detached himself from the shadows, glided over and assisted her to her place. Kassim seated himself directly opposite and grinned. 'You seem surprised, Janene. Did you imagine we'd be squatting on a carpet, eating from a bowl with our fingers? Perhaps being offered a sheep's eye as a delicacy?'

She swallowed. 'If you're trying to put me off my food, you're going the right way about it.' She watched him sip his wine, then frowned. 'I thought Muslims weren't supposed to take alcohol?'

'They aren't,' he conceded patiently. 'But then, I'm a weak, vacillating fool of a man. I shall atone for my sins in some suitable manner and pray for forgiveness. Meanwhile, why don't you sample yours and tell me what you think of my cellar?'

She raised her glass to her lips and eyed him warily over the rim. There was nothing weak about him, she told herself. Cautiously she took a sip. . .then another. Putting the glass down on the table, she gave her verdict. 'It's a bit like you. Overpowering.'

He laughed in pleasure. 'And it's sweet,' he added. 'Just like you. A good combination. You and I will blend well together. I think we were made for each other. You shall be the jewelled sheath for my sword.'

In the candlelight his eyes seemed to glow as if lit from inside, and her hand trembled ever so slightly as she reached for the glass again.

The main course was a dish of tender chicken pieces which had been marinated and served with a delicious lemon sauce. At her first taste, she opened her eyes and nodded. 'This is nice!'

'It should be,' he said drily. 'I stole my chef from one of the best hotels in Paris.'

'Really?' She raised a mocking eyebrow. 'Is he the

miserable wretch you were threatening to have flogged this morning?'

'The very one,' he replied lightly. 'You've no idea how relieved he was when I told him that you'd enjoyed your breakfast.'

She pierced another piece of chicken with her fork and gave him a cold smile. 'You seem to make a habit of stealing whatever you want. First your chef. And then me.'

Their eyes clashed for a moment and, as she looked away, he grinned. 'Louis isn't complaining. He's only working half as hard for twice the money. He likes it here. Just as I'm sure you'll learn to like it.'

She lowered her head and finished her meal in discreet silence. She always seemed to come off worst in these verbal skirmishes, and the mere act of looking into those electric-blue eyes weakened any resolve she was able to muster.

Arming himself with another bottle and fresh glasses, he led her out into the courtyard. The scent of flowers was heavy in the warm night air, and the calm waters of the pool reflected the light from a thousand stars.

Stopping by a marble balustrade, he poured some more wine and raised his glass in a toast. 'Here's to our first night together, Janene,' he said softly. 'May it be one to shake the earth from its orbit.'

There was a husky tremor in her voice as she stared up at him. 'You're quite an incredible man, Kassim! You have the nerve to ask me to drink to my own seduction!'

'Why not?' he murmured. 'You can hardly wait, can you? I can feel the wild beat of your heart vibrating in the very air that surrounds us.'

'You're too damned sure of yourself,' she muttered resentfully. 'That wild beating you hear might be fear, or panic.'

His voice gently mocked her. 'If you do fear anything, it's not me. It's the raging demon of desire within yourself. You're afraid it will get loose and out of control.'

She bit her lip and looked away, not even attempting to deny something that she was becoming more acutely aware of by the minute. There was something about this man—a force as invisible yet as irresistible as the moon that pulled at the tides. From the moment of their first meeting at the party, when those compelling blue eyes had drilled into hers, she'd wanted him. Oh, she hadn't dared admit it to herself at the time. Denied it, even. But it had all been an act, and it was no use pretending any longer. Her body was aching. She needed him.

As if sensing her readiness, he took her left hand and pressed it to his lips, then murmured, 'During dinner I noticed that you'd removed your ring. I hope you weren't motivated by a sense of guilt in the knowledge that you'd decided to betray your fiancé?'

'I—I gave it to Kebira,' she stammered, her mouth dry and her legs weak. 'I told her to keep it. It's all over between Damien and me.'

His lips drew back, baring his teeth in a satisfied smile. 'A wise decision, Janene. I knew my ineffable charm would win you over in the end.'

'It hasn't got anything to do with you or your ineffable charm,' she informed him quietly.

He grinned and reached for her. 'We'll talk about it after we've entered the gates of paradise.'

It was the casual presumption implicit in that single action which rekindled her flame of anger. He'd succeeded in exposing a dark and wanton side to her nature—something she'd never been aware of until now, something that filled her with guilt and created a conflict of emotions.

But it was the cavalier way he was treating her which rankled most of all. Only a matter of hours ago, he'd snatched her from her cottage, and, despite her protests on the plane, had brought her here. And now he thought that he merely had to snap his fingers and she'd leap into bed with him! If that proved anything at all, it merely went to show how much respect he had for her.

She pushed his hand away and said hotly, 'You're taking too damned much for granted.'

His blue eyes hardened, but she stared right back at him defiantly.

His eyes continued to clash with hers, then his mouth quirked. 'There is a look of hurt dignity on your face, Janene. If I've said anything to offend you, then you have my humble apologies.'

'It isn't what you say,' she retorted irritably. 'It—it's the way you go about things. All that power has gone to your head. You see something you want, and you think you have the god-given right to take it.'

He considered her statement thoughtfully, then shrugged. 'That's us hot-blooded foreigners for you. Unlike you English, we're not ashamed of our appetites and we take our pleasure where and when we can. Life is too short to waste time.'

'Observing the rules of decency is never a waste of time,' she pointed out coldly.

He looked puzzled for a moment, then he gave an

understanding nod. 'You're still angry at the way you were brought here. Is that it?'

'It'll do for a start,' she muttered.

'Or could it be resentment at me for telling you that Damien was involved in drugs?' he suggested, with a hint of cynicism. 'You still think that I'm making it up?'

She shook her head, and confessed bitterly, 'I didn't believe you at first. Now. . .well, I'm not so sure. You're many things, but I don't think you're a liar.' Only people who had something to hide, or were afraid, ever needed to resort to lies. Kassim struck her as the kind of man who was afraid of nothing.

'Thanks for the vote of confidence,' he murmured drily. He refilled her glass and led her firmly by the arm over to the couch by the side of the pool. At her look of suspicion, he allayed her fears with a friendly smile. 'Don't worry. You and I are merely going to sit and talk for a while.'

She clutched her glass and tried to stop her hand from trembling. She'd gladly sit up all night and talk, if that was all he wanted.

He eased himself on to the couch beside her, sitting sideways, not touching her but subjecting her to a gaze of penetrating intensity. 'You're the most exciting woman I've ever met, Janene, and I want to know all about you. Yet you're still a mystery to me. I know nothing of you, the way your mind works.'

'There's nothing wrong with the way my mind works,' she told him shakily. 'You're probably so used to women throwing themselves at your feet that when you meet one who won't——'

He held up a hand to stifle her angry outburst. 'I admire a woman of principle, Janene. I wouldn't be interested in you otherwise.' He stopped and studied her in genuine puzzlement. 'Damien is a nasty piece of work. I can't imagine what you ever saw in him. But your sudden decision to end your association with him would imply that you at least suspected him of something. Did you?'

The question brought a flush of resentment to her face and she snapped, 'Of course not! As far as I knew, he was a self-employed financial adviser. He never gave me any reason to think otherwise.' She bit her lip. 'I was a fool. I thought that I was in love with him, but I came to realise. . .' She swallowed the painful lump in her throat as the memories of that terrible day re-emerged from the depths of her mind to torment her.

Suddenly her self-control snapped and she dropped her glass and buried her face in her hands. Vaguely she was aware of Kassim's comforting arm round her shoulder and his voice whispering tenderly in her ear, 'Tell me what troubles you, little rose. Your heart is heavy. Let me share your burden.'

# CHAPTER FIVE

WITH a final shudder, Janene managed to regain her self-control. She lowered her hands to her lap and stared at them in miserable silence. Kassim's arm was still round her shoulder but she made no attempt to shake it off. On the contrary, she found it strangely comforting.

'Go on,' he urged softly. 'Share your pain with me. If Damien ever hurt you. . .'

'No,' she said dully. 'It was all my fault. I never really loved Damien. I know that now. It—it was something that Sally said that brought me to my senses.'

Sensing her reluctance to go on, he prodded her gently. 'Who is Sally?'

'A girl back in London,' she explained quietly. 'We were in business together once.'

'What kind of business?' he enquired, not giving her the chance to retreat into an introverted silence.

'We—we owned a string of boutiques,' she explained, finding it easier to talk now. 'We specialised in fashion jewellery. We were making quite a success of it. I know that sounds conceited, but it's true.'

'You'd be a success at anything you put your mind to,' he said gallantly.

Her green eyes misted at the memory. 'Oh, yes. I was proud of what I'd achieved. At last I had my independence. But unfortunately my parents didn't see it that way. They'd much rather have seen me settling down and raising a family.'

'An ambition most caring parents have,' he pointed out quietly.

She bowed her head again. 'Yes. I knew only too well that I was a disappointment to them. I tried to make it up to them by sending them on a luxury holiday. I—I drove them to the airport. . .watched the plane take off. . .' The words tumbled from her mouth as she described the scene—the sights and sounds that had haunted her ever since.

One moment the plane had been soaring gracefully into the air. Suddenly it had dipped. A wing-tip had struck the ground. . .Then the massive fireball of flame and twisted metal cartwheeling down the runway. The shocked, numbed silence. Then the screaming and the wailing of rescue vehicles and fire-engines. . .

By the time she'd finished the story her brow was damp with perspiration and she felt as weak as someone whose fever had at last broken. But, strangely enough, her mind felt clearer now that the poison had been purged from her system.

'So that is the burden you have been carrying in your heart,' Kassim said softly.

She nodded and closed her eyes. 'They'd never have been on that plane if it hadn't been for me.'

He took one of her hands in his and soothed her gently. 'Your feelings of guilt are understandable, but foolish, Janene. Our destinies are in the hands of fate. Not you, nor I, nor any mere mortal can alter that. And one should never be haunted by the ghosts of the past. Each day in one's life should be a fresh, unblemished page upon which to leave your mark.'

'Yes. . .' she said wearily. 'It's easy to think like that with hindsight. But at the time I was too numb with shock to be so rational. All I could think of was some way of making it up to my parents. They—they'd always wanted me to marry, settle down and raise a family, so that's exacly what I set out to do. I sold my half of the business to Sally and waited for the right man to come along.' She gave a snort of self-deprecation. 'No. Let's be truthful. Any man. Just so long as he was reasonably attractive and successful. I met Damien at a party and he seemed to fit the bill. The rest is history. I pretended to myself that it was love, but I think I always knew deep in my heart that it wasn't the real thing.'

'But he was the price you were willing to pay in order to atone for your imagined sins,' Kassim muttered, revealing an insight that surprised her. Even more surprising was the look of dismal self-reproach on his face as he added bitterly, 'Now I understand your anger at me. With such tribulation to bear, the last thing you need is a swaggering fool such as I barging into your life and making it even more complicated.'

As he made to rise she felt a new emotion creeping into her heart, and she restrained him gently. 'Please don't blame yourself, Kassim. You weren't to know.' She looked into his tortured blue eyes and smiled. 'Perhaps you were exactly what I needed. I've never been able to talk to anyone about it before. Now that you've helped me bring it out into the open, I feel better.'

A tiny shiver ran through her as he kissed her tenderly on the forehead. The sharing of her innermost secret had lightened her heart and drawn him closer.

He was no longer a threat. He was a rock on which to lean and shelter.

'You need a good night's sleep,' he said gravely. 'I'll tell Kebira to prepare another room for you.'

This manifestation of the thoughtfulness behind his remark completed the slow and subtle change of her feelings for him and, making a conscious decision, she looked directly into his eyes and whispered, 'That won't be necessary, Kassim.'

The lighting in the room was subdued, a mere rose-coloured glow that did nothing to diminish the brilliance of the stars as Kassim threw open the shutters. A slice of moon hung motionless, like the spinnaker sail of some ghostly yacht crossing the infinities of space.

He had carried her up from the courtyard below, cradled in his strong arms like a child, and now she stood where he'd put her down, her insides dissolving and her heart fluttering like a bird in a cage as he turned from the window and glided towards her.

She was seized by a sudden feeling of panic. Had she made the right decision? Were the feelings he aroused in her sufficient reason for what she was about to let happen? Was she really falling in love with him or was it only a knee-jerk response to his words of tenderness? And what about him? What were his true feelings towards her?

In a hypnotic daze, she stared up into the luminosity of those eyes as he put his hands gently on her shoulders and murmured down at her, 'I've longed for this moment, little rose. Do you remember what I told you when we first met?'

She managed to unstick her tongue from the roof of

her mouth. 'No. You—you said such a lot.' She'd never felt as feverishly excited as this before. Even the seductive sound of his deep, masculine voice was bringing her out in bumps.

'Then I'll remind you,' he said hoarsely in her ear. 'I told you that I'd strip away that shell of cold reserve and release a storm of fire and passion. Well, that shell is beginning to crack and I can feel the heat already.'

Cupping her face in his hands possessively, he lowered his mouth slowly on to hers and teased her lips apart with his tongue. A tiny moan bubbled in her throat and her hands impulsively clutched at his waist.

His tongue continued its invasion and her moan grew in tortured intensity. Her hands, seemingly endowed with a life of their own, reached up frantically to entwine themselves in his thick, dark hair.

Gently he detached himself from her and held her at arm's length for a moment while his eyes savoured her in anticipation. 'Sex is an art, little rose,' he mouthed huskily. 'And, like art, it should never be hurried. Each brush-stroke must be thought out and then executed with slow deliberation. But the first requirement is a good canvas to work on. I must see and study that canvas before I begin work.'

Through eyes hot and heavy-lidded with desire, she saw him remove the silver clip from her robe. Now was the time to put an end to this. All she needed to do was summon up the will-power to say, 'Enough!'

Her robe fell open and it was too late. Under its own weight it slipped from her shoulders and whispered over her smooth, creamy skin to drift down to the floor, leaving her exposed in nothing but flimsy bra and briefs.

As she saw the hot, smoky desire come to his eyes,

she was seized by a heady feeling of liberation, as if some invisible chain inside her had snapped. Why should she feel ashamed of her nakedness when the sight of it was having such an obvious effect on him? For the first time in her life, she understood the relationship between power and sex. Sex didn't have to mean submission. It could be the power to give or withhold pleasure.

Watching him carefully, revelling in every nuance of changing expression on his dark and mobile features, she slowly removed her bra and stepped out of her briefs. In the silence of the room she heard the sharp intake of his breath. Slowly, he spread his arms wide and uttered a harsh command, 'Come to me, Janene.'

She was hardly conscious of her feet on the ground as she stepped forward.

'Now undress me,' he said thickly.

Stepping back slightly, she smiled up at him through half-closed eyes and murmured softly, 'I've never undressed a man before. You'll have to help me.'

Grinning in anticipation, he loosened the belt on his tunic and it opened to reveal his loose cotton shirt.

'So many buttons,' she whispered. 'This could take all night.'

Gently he placed her hand on the top button and smiled darkly. 'We've got all night. Take your time.'

She worked her fingers slowly downwards, then slipped the open garment over his shoulders. As his hard-muscled chest was exposed she was driven by her own sensual desire to brush her lips over both his nipples. He tasted sweet and smelt of fresh soap, and she traced her fingertips over his smooth, velvety skin.

Hungry for more of his magnificent body, she slowly

sank to her knees and undid the belt at his waist. She could hear his breath rasping above her as she completed his undressing, and her own breathing became tight and heavy as his manhood was revealed, proud and arrogantly poised.

Rising to her feet, she gazed into his eyes, her mouth ready and eager for his. His arms enfolded her and the heat of their passion seemed to fuse their flesh together. With his lips only inches from hers, he looked deeply into her eyes and whispered hoarsely, 'By the beard of Shaitan, Janene, women with only half your delectable charm and beauty have driven men mad with lust, and started wars.'

She looped her arms round his neck and breathed up at him, 'I thought the idea was to make love, not war, Kassim. Isn't that what you want?'

His mouth came down on hers, hard and bruising, and answering her question with its hungry demand. Every soft contour of her body was pressed hard against him, her breasts flattened and his knee thrusting between her thighs. Suddenly he relaxed his hold on her long enough to sweep her up into his arms and carry her over to the bed. Laying her down gently, he straightened up and stood over her like some mountain warrior surveying the lush valley he was about to invade.

She reached up for him imploringly, but he calmed her in a deep, soothing voice. 'Patience, my little rose. Our eyes must have their fill before we proceed to the other senses.'

Her eyes were undoubtedly getting their fill of him as the shadows played across the hard, corded thighs and flat stomach.

Finally he drew a deep, satisfied breath and lay down beside her. Tenderly he touched each pink and swollen nipple, then took one in his mouth. A soft moan of indescribable pleasure escaped her lips and she clutched feverishly at his hair. His hand slowly moved down her body and her flesh jumped and quivered as his fingertips traced tiny circles, lower and lower, until she writhed in an abandoned ecstasy when he reached between her thighs.

Now her nails were digging into his back and her breathing was hot and rapid. As he began a slow, erotic massage with his fingers, her body arched upwards and she gasped his name over and over again. Then, almost at the incandescent apex of her arousal, he rolled gently on top of her. With eyes dilated hugely, she gazed up into his face and bit her lip to stifle her moan of passion as he slowly but inexorably entered her.

Supporting his own weight with the palms of his hands by her shoulders, he smiled down at her in delight and murmured, 'So warm. So sweet. So snug. It has truly found a fitting home at last.'

Completely enslaved by the unremitting demands of her own body, she began to squirm beneath him until, amused at her impatience, he took up the initiative and began thrusting himself deep and rhythmically.

The intense excitation galvanised her into wrapping her legs round his waist and clawing at his back. His thrusting drove her ever upwards until she reached a shuddering climax, and she bit into his shoulder to stifle the cries and groans of sublime sexual fulfilment.

Gasping and wet with perspiration, she clung to him until the tremors in her body subsided, then, pulling

Kassim's head down, she kissed him and said throatily, 'That was wonderful.'

'Was?' One of his dark eyebrows was raised and she saw the intense glint in his eyes. 'But, *chérie*,' he murmured deeply, 'we are not yet finished.'

Her eyes widened in surprise as he began to move inside her again. 'What the——?' His mouth dropped on hers again and her own body joined in the rhythm. Then, as his movement became faster and more urgent, she again experienced that heart-stopping anticipation. She heard him emit a deep groan of pleasure, and at the moment of his hot, flooding release she reached a second climax.

For a second time her body fell into a state of euphoric exhaustion.

He rolled off her and lay on his side, smiling at her lazily. 'Well, little rose? Did I make you happy?'

She'd got her breath back by now but her voice was still a hoarse croak as she said, 'Twice! I can't believe it!'

He propped himself up on one elbow and traced his fingers over her upper thigh. 'Discipline and training,' he drawled. 'That's all it takes.'

She opened one eye and queried with a slight frown, 'Training?'

He laughed softly at her expression. 'In our tribe, boys are trained at puberty. They are taught restraint. If a man cannot satisfy a woman he is not considered worthy of the name.'

She was about to ask him who the lucky girl he'd practised on was, then decided that he might take offence. Instead she commented innocently, 'A man like you must have had many women. . .' She paused, then added quickly, 'In the cause of research, of course.'

He bent his head and kissed her lightly. 'Your bantering tone doesn't fool me, Janene. There is more behind that question than you'd dare to admit.'

'I—I'm not sure I know what you're getting at,' she faltered.

'It is of no matter,' he said casually. 'But the answer to your question is no. I am very particular about the women I choose. Sex is a pleasure which should not be indulged in indiscriminately.'

The answer pleased her. It was always possible that he was simply being sensitive to her feelings, but she didn't think so. He was, she reminded herself, not the kind of man to lie about anything.

After a while a delicious warmth stole over her and she closed her eyes. His lips touched hers again briefly, and she heard him murmur, 'Sleep well, little rose. You have earned your rest.'

That was easier said than done. Time and again she was jerked back from the edge of oblivion by tiny voices raising doubts and asking questions. Kassim was having no such problems and, as she listened to his deep, relaxed breathing, she knew without the slightest doubt that she was in love with him, and she also realised that she could be making the biggest mistake of her life.

She would gladly spend the rest of her days with him, but what were his plans for her? She was worldly enough to know that most men didn't equate sex with true love. They derided the idea that having sex with a woman gave her the right to throw a halter round his neck.

It was hard to believe that he'd just brought her here to save her from getting involved with the police. After all, why should he go to all that trouble over a stranger?

The only other possibility was that all he felt for her was a strong, physical attraction and he got some sort of kick from having her in his power. When she'd first met him at the party, she'd made it quite clear that she had no intention of going to Morocco with him, so he'd resorted to the old tradition of abduction. His action could have been born of sheer impetuosity, and who was to say how long the mood would last? In a week's time she might well find herself being returned to England as unceremoniously as she'd been brought here.

At last she did succumb to sleep. The questions would have to wait

'I trust that you slept well last night?' he asked politely, over breakfast at the poolside table the following morning.

Janene met the amused glitter in his eye with a wry smile. 'Very well.'

'Good,' he murmured. 'I can think of no pleasanter way of exhausting oneself. We'll indulge in some more. . .exercise tonight.'

She sipped her coffee and watched him demolish a segment of orange.

'Sister Mary will be here shortly,' he informed her casually. 'She will chaperon you if you wish to go into town. Unfortunately I must attend to business again today. But tomorrow I am taking you on a trip to see the Blue Men.'

'Blue Men?' she asked, raising her brows in amusement. 'Who are they?'

'Men of my tribe who live in the desert,' he said carelessly. 'They are very astute traders. They'll examine you and tell me if I got my money's worth.'

She looked at him sharply, then relaxed. She was getting used to his dry, ironic sense of humour by now; otherwise she might have asked him to explain exactly what he meant by that remark.

Kebira had been hovering nearby in attendance, and Kassim beckoned her over and spoke to her quietly in Arabic.

As soon as the servant-girl had hurried back into the house he said, 'You may want to purchase something in the market. I've sent Kebira to fetch some money. And it would be wise to take her into town with you. She's an astute girl and she'll see that you're not cheated.'

She glanced at the pool and said wistfully, 'I don't suppose they sell swimsuits at the market?' She'd heard tales about tourists in Arab countries being pelted with stones for daring to walk along a beach in a scanty bikini.

'There are plenty of swimsuits in the house. Just ask Kebira to fetch you one.' He grinned. 'You needn't bother about wearing anything if you want to make use of this pool, however. No one will be permitted to see you. Apart from myself, that is. In fact, I may join you.'

'Yes. . .' she murmured. 'I thought you'd come up with an idea like that.' She sipped her coffee, then put her cup down carefully. She wasn't taking any more chances with handles coming off.

The sound of a horn announced Sister Mary's arrival

in the outer courtyard, and five minutes later Janene was in the passenger seat of the Jeep, with Kebira in the rear, heading into town.

Mary parked the Jeep and they proceeded on foot into the noisy bustle of the souk. There was a half-formed idea in Janene's head, and she decided that today she was going to go through this market with a fine-tooth comb to see what exactly was on offer and how much it cost. Her primary interest was in the jewellery, but she'd be on the look-out for anything else that took her fancy.

As they entered the maze of narrow alleyways she turned to Mary. 'Who are the Blue Men? Kassim is taking me to see them tomorrow.'

Mary gave her a peculiar look, then murmured, 'Is he, indeed? Now, that's interesting, to be sure.' She seemed to be on the point of expanding on that remark, then she changed her mind and said glibly, 'Sure, and they're tall, handsome, swaggering devils, just like Kassim. Terrible for fighting in the old days, I believe. They wear blue cloaks and black turbans drawn across their faces like a veil. I've treated some at the clinic. Broken bones, mostly. They don't talk much except among themselves, but they've never given me any trouble.'

Janene looked at her thoughtfully. 'Why do you think Kassim wants me to meet them?'

Mary shrugged. 'He probably thinks you'd be interested in seeing how they live out in the desert. They have to be tough to survive out there.'

She left it at that. Mary was probably right. Just so long as Kassim didn't have any funny ideas about trading her to a bunch of Arabs for a few camels and a bag of silver, she thought with wry amusement.

They'd only gone another few yards when the skin on the back of her neck began to prickle, and she glanced over her shoulder in time to see the man side-step and disappear into an alley. He'd been quick, but not quite quick enough, and for an instant their eyes had met, sending a shiver through her. The hatred in those glittering eyes, the livid scar down one cheek, the dirty turban and robe. . .

For a moment she stared at the mouth of the alley, wondering if the whole thing had been a product of her overwrought imagination, then Mary was looking at her in alarm and asking what was wrong.

'Nothing,' she muttered. Pulling herself together, she managed a smile. 'It's just the heat, I suppose.' Pushing the incident from her mind, she followed Mary and Kebira deeper into the souk.

Suddenly a blaze of colour caught her eye and she stopped at the display of colourful waistcoats. It was the rich-looking embroidery that fascinated her, and the stallholder, spotting a potential customer and eager for a sale, thrust one into her hands with a broad, oily smile and a torrent of Arabic. Turning to Mary, she said, 'Ask him how much he wants for this.'

Before Mary could open her mouth, Kebira pushed herself forward, took the garment from her mistress's hands and examined it briefly. Contemptuously, she tossed it back at the trader and spoke to him sharply. He answered equally sharply, and with seconds there was a first-rate slanging match in progress.

Taken by surprise, Janene turned to Mary. 'What on earth is going on?'

Mary sighed. 'It's awful. I've never heard such language. Kebira has just called him a fat, blood-sucking leech to be selling such rubbish. And then he called a plague of boils upon her head and hoped that all her children would be girls with warts on their noses, and anyway, all his wares were guaranteed, and Kebira said, "Yes. Guaranteed to fall to bits after the first wash." And now he's telling her——'

'Never mind,' Janene said hastily. 'I get the picture. Let's move on.'

They extricated Kebira from the argument and led her away. Mary questioned Kebira, then explained, 'She says that he was lying. They are not made here. They are cheap, inferior waistcoats imported from Portugal. He pays the women here a pittance for embroidering them. She says that the wool is chemically dyed and will soon fade. The spinners here use veg-etable dyes, which they make themselves from madder-roots and the indigo-plant. She insists that she knows where to get the real thing.'

'Does she, indeed?' Janene regarded Kebira with keen interest, then said, 'Ask her if she knows where I can get some really good hand-crafted jewellery, like those bangles we saw yesterday.'

Kebira, subdued and seemingly embarrassed by her presumptuous behaviour, listened as Mary put the question, then she nodded excitedly and replied with much arm-waving and gesticulation.

Mary translated. 'She says that she knows many fine silversmiths who make lovely brooches and ear-rings.'

With barely controlled excitement, Janene gave the startled girl a hug and said happily, '*Très bon*, Kebira. *Vous êtes une petite*. . .goldmine. *Je suis très* proud of *vous*. Can *vous*. . .er. . .take us. . .show us? *Je* must *regarder les* jewellery.'

Kebira, getting the gist of the request, bobbed her head and smiled shyly. '*Mais oui, madame*.' She began walking in the lead, beckoning them to follow.

The souk was far too large and congested to cover in one visit, and Janene knew it would take a few more days to see everything. Kebira seemed to know every inch of the place, outside and in. At first she led them down a narrow alley crammed with vendors and selling spices, powders, cooking-oil, pots and pans. There were little nook-in-the-wall restaurants with people laughing or arguing good-naturedly over bowls of soup. Right next to one, a blacksmith was fitting new shoes to a patient mule. Then suddenly Kebira led them into another, smaller alleyway, and through a doorway into a tiny courtyard, where two old men and a young woman stood by a glowing brazier and a work-bench, making silver filigree ear-rings. Janene picked up one sample and knew she'd hit the jackpot.

Four hours later she'd acquired two leather hold-alls filled with samples of the local jewellery, leatherwork, and garments. After a meal at a small but clean restaurant, they made their way back through the souk towards the Jeep.

They were about halfway there when the skin on the back of her neck began to prickle again. She stopped abruptly, turned and stared back into the sea of faces.

Mary looked at her in alarm. 'Is anything wrong?'

Her eyes continued to search the crowd, then she muttered, 'It—it's nothing.' How could you explain a feeling? A feeling that your every movement was being watched? 'Nothing,' she repeated. 'Just imagination.'

# CHAPTER SIX

DIRECTLY after breakfast the following morning, Kassim began preparations for their visit to the Blue Men. The four-wheel-drive vehicle was checked for fuel and oil, and two five-gallon kegs of fresh drinking-water were loaded into the back. There was also, to Janene's surprise, a huge crate of tinned food, and she wondered how long this trip was going to take. At least a month, by the look of it!

The road out of town to the east was smooth for the first mile, then it became more and more rutted and finally disappeared altogether. She pulled down the sun-visor, stared through the windscreen at the bleak landscape ahead, and suppressed a shudder. At the wheel of the Land Rover, Kassim looked sideways and grinned at her. 'Welcome to the real Morocco.'

There was nothing to be seen but sunbaked red earth, tortured rocks and a few stunted, arthritic trees. Heat rose in shimmering waves, distorting distances, and she was glad of the air-conditioning. Those rocks out there looked hot enough to fry an egg. 'Do people actually live out here?' she asked in awe.

He gave a brief nod. 'Many. Some people don't like cities.'

'Well. . .I'm not that keen on them myself,' she admitted ruefully. 'But I don't think I'd give them up for this.'

He dropped a gear, carefully choosing his route

between the scattered rocks and obstacles, and she relapsed into silence, allowing him to concentrate on his driving.

Last night their lovemaking had been even more adventurous and just as enthusiastic as the night before, and there was no reason to suppose that the same thing wouldn't happen tonight. But the question she'd been worrying about still remained unanswered.

It was obvious that, the longer she stayed here with this enigmatic man, the deeper she was getting in love. If only she could have sustained her initial anger against him instead of falling prey to her own desires, she wouldn't be in this mess now. They all said that falling in love was wonderful, but none of them ever got around to mentioning all the problems and heartaches it caused.

There had to be some way of finding out his intentions. She shrank from the idea of forcing the issue by asking him directly. That would be too blatantly obvious. But surely there had to be another way.

There were about another ten miles of rough terrain until the land changed from red earth to well-packed sand. They passed the crumbling ruins of a fort, parts of its limewashed crenellated walls still standing, where the ghosts of long-dead *légionnaires* looked down at them over rifle-sights. Beyond the fort stretched an endless sea of sand and dunes. Kassim kept driving.

Judging it safe to speak now, she glanced at him. 'Would you like to answer a question that's been bothering me?'

His blue eyes looked sideways at her. 'Certainly. You are wondering if we are lost?'

The thought had never entered her mind. He was the

last man on earth she'd have expected to get himself lost. He probably knew every grain of sand out here by its first and second name.

'No,' she said quietly. 'I've been wondering how you managed to sneak me out of England, without my passport, aboard a private plane. I thought all flights in and out of a country had to be cleared by the authorities. Customs and people like that? I suppose you managed to bribe someone? I mean. . .it's the kind of thing your ancestors went in for, isn't it? Bribery and corruption.'

His eyes flickered over her dangerously, then he grunted, 'Sometimes it is better to remain in ignorance of the ways of the world. Especially if you are a woman.'

She looked at him in resentment. 'Don't be so patronising. I've answered your questions. You could at least be courteous enough to answer mine.' She averted her eyes from his stern features and examined the landscape again. 'You've treated me well and I wouldn't repay you by reporting your misdemeanours to the authorities, so you needn't worry about that.'

He gave her a thin, ironic smile. 'Thank you. I will rest easier in my bed at night now.'

His sarcasm grated across her nerves and she said crossly, 'All right! Forget I ever asked.' She folded her arms, pouted her lips angrily and stared straight ahead in silence.

He eyed her in exasperation, then said, 'Do you know what kef is?'

'No.' She kept staring ahead, still annoyed with him.

'It's marijuana,' he explained patiently. 'A lot of it is grown in Morocco, smuggled into Spain and ends up in

England. In the past I have worked closely with your Customs people to stop this evil traffic. In return they allow me a little latitude in my travel arrangements.'

'That must be convenient,' she observed tartly. She was going to leave it at that, when she suddenly realised that this was the very opening she'd been looking for. Making her voice as casual as possible, she remarked, 'So I can take it that there'll be no problems taking me back home?'

He looked as if he'd just been bitten by a snake, and he turned on her. 'You have been my guest for little more than two days, and already you speak about leaving!'

His angry reaction took her by surprise, and she stammered, 'I—I didn't mean it like that. I'll stay just as long as you want me to.'

He went on as if he hadn't heard a word she had said. 'In this country we pride ourselves on our hospitality, and in less enlightened company your remark would be regarded as a personal insult to your host.'

'All right,' she complained. 'Don't go over the top.'

He looked at her suspiciously. 'Perhaps you grow tired of my lovemaking?'

She gulped in embarrassment. 'I—I've no complaints about that,' she assured him hastily. 'You're an absolute gold-medallist in bed. An absolute demon. A—a veritable——'

'Be careful,' he growled in warning. 'I'm the one who goes in for the flowery language. It doesn't ring true coming from the lips of a red-haired Anglo-Saxon.' He paused, then added drily, 'Perhaps I don't come up to the demanding standards set by your ex-lovers?'

She looked at him indignantly and snapped, 'I don't have any ex-lovers.'

He raised a mocking eyebrow. 'What about Damien?'

She sighed in exasperation. 'All right! One ex-lover.' She looked directly into those questioning eyes and said quietly, 'My past life has nothing to do with you, Kassim, but I've nothing to hide. Damien and I made love a few times. At least, I thought that was what we were doing. But I didn't know any better until I met you. I always thought that it was simply a matter of the woman pleasing the man. You taught me differently.'

She turned to stare through the windscreen again. If that little speech didn't soothe his ego, then nothing would. Anyway, now she had a partial answer to her question. She was nothing more than a 'guest' here. Her spirits began to sink.

They'd been travelling in silence for another fifteen minutes when she became aware of the sudden change in the lighting. Ever since they'd left the town the sun had been beating down mercilessly from a cloudless sky, but now there was an ominous brassy tinge that threw the landscape into sharp relief. The effect was eerie. The sun darkened and then the very air seemed to turn brown.

Kassim pressed hard on the pedal and grunted, 'Sandstorm coming.' There was a large dune directly ahead of them, and as he detoured round it her eyes opened wide in horror. An enormous black wall about a mile high was racing across the desert towards them.

'It's nothing to worry about,' he said confidently. 'We'll park here and sit it out.'

Dry-mouthed, she watched the rapidly approaching

storm, then said tremulously, 'Wouldn't we be better sheltering behind the dune?'

'If we do we'll be buried alive.' He gave her a thin smile. 'What's wrong, Janene? I've said that it's nothing to worry about. Don't you trust me?'

She looked at him helplessly, her knuckles white in her lap, then she looked at the advancing nightmare, then she looked back at him, and gulped and nodded. 'Y—yes, Kassim.'

He switched off the engine. 'Good. Just make sure that all the windows on your side are closed tight.'

Thirty seconds later, the storm hit them. The Land Rover gave a sickening lurch, as if it had been struck by a huge fist, and day turned to night. There was a roaring sound as tons of wind-driven sand battered and scoured the vehicle. In a panic, she threw herself into the safety of Kassim's arms and buried her face in his chest like a frightened child.

Protectively his arm went round her, and over the noise of the storm his voice whispered in her ear, 'Don't be afraid, little rose. It is only wind and sand. It cannot harm us in here.'

She looked up at him in the darkness, and her voice quavered, 'How—how long will it last?'

'That is in the hands of Allah. Perhaps minutes. Perhaps days, if someone has greatly offended Him.'

Days. . .? Oh, my God! she thought. They couldn't spend days cooped up in here! She blinked as he reached up and switched on the interior light. The very air inside the vehicle was filled with a fine, gritty dust that she tasted in her mouth and felt burning her eyes.

Kassim had drawn his robe tighter and pulled his turban across his face like a mask, and he carefully rearranged her headscarf in the same manner. 'Now do you see the reason for the way we dress in the desert?' he asked. 'It's protection against the elements. Sun, sand and wind.'

Slowly regaining her poise, she sat up. With Kassim by her side she was more fascinated than frightened now.

'What happens if you're caught out in the open in a storm like this?' she asked, wide-eyed.

'Just do what your camel does and you'll be perfectly safe,' he assured her. 'Lie down beside it with your back to the wind and pull your robe over your head.'

Having offered her that handy piece of advice, he clambered over his seat and rummaged around in the back. A moment later he thrust a mug of cold water into her hand. 'Drink this. It'll wash the dust from your mouth.'

After the drink she felt calmer, and she looked at him quizzically. 'You must have expected something like this. That's why you brought all the food and water, isn't it? We might be stuck here for days, as you said.'

He shook his head and explained patiently, 'The food is a present for my friends. Delicacies they seldom see. As for the water—only a fool travels in the desert without more than enough to spare. As for the storms. . .they move too quickly to be predicted.'

'Oh, I see.' It was just dawning on her how out of her depth she was. Everything was so alien to her previous experiences. 'I'm sorry for asking all these stupid questions.'

'Don't be, ' he said generously. 'It's only by asking questions that one learns. Stiff-necked pride merely leads to ignorance. To someone used to the civilised English countryside, all this must seem strange.'

She handed him back the mug. 'Strange isn't the word for it.' She looked at the darkened windscreen and heard the screech of the wind, then said fervently, 'No one's ever going to get me within a hundred miles of a desert after this.'

He shrugged. 'I'm sorry you're being subjected to this ordeal, but I'm afraid it was a journey that had to be undertaken. It's a matter of honour and tradition, you understand?'

She frowned at him. 'No. I'm afraid I don't understand.' Suddenly she remembered what he'd told her yesterday about the Blue Men examining her to see what she was worth. At the time, she'd dismissed it as one of his jokes, but suppose he'd been serious!

With hard suspicion in her eyes and grim determination in her voice, she challenged him. 'Before we go any further I think you'd better explain in straightforward English just why you're taking me to see your friends. And I don't want to hear any more about "honour" and "tradition". Your honour didn't prevent you from snatching me from my home and, for all I know, it might be a "tradition" here for you to share me among your friends.' She took a deep breath and glared at him. 'Unless you swear to me that I'm not going to wake up tomorrow morning in some strange Arab's tent, I'm going to open this door and take my chances outside.' To emphasise the threat, she grabbed the door-handle.

His hand clamped around her arm and he looked into her eyes intensely. 'You really would, wouldn't you?'

'Damn right I would,' she said defiantly, trying to tug her arm free.

He continued to stare at her, his blue eyes faintly puzzled, then he released her and gave a crooked smile. 'Relax, Janene. For what it's worth, you have my word that no harm will befall you.'

'Yes,' she muttered, only half convinced by his assurance. 'You'd rather be cast naked into a pit of scorpions. I've heard it before.'

For a moment he sat in tight-lipped silence, deep in thought, casting her occasional sidelong glances. Finally he came to his decision. 'Very well! Since I don't have your complete trust, we will turn round and go back as soon as the storm is over.'

Good! she thought. That suited her fine. She'd never wanted to come on this trip in the first place. Again she pouted her lips, folded her arms across her chest, and tried to ignore him.

Her conscience began to prick her, faintly at first. She tried to ignore that as well, but it just got worse. Wasn't she being just a little bit hysterical over this business? she asked herself. She remembered the way he'd dealt with the case of the divorced women. He'd shown compassion and a deep sense of justice. Was it likely that a man with these qualities would go back on his word? The whole thing could really be quite innocent, and her irrational fears were denying him the right to visit his friends and relatives. Dammit! No wonder she was being irrational. It was this hellish storm that was affecting her mind.

Slowly the noise of the wind diminished and the darkness outside lightened to a dim yellow, then, as suddenly as it had disappeared, the sun blazed down from a bright sky.

They both climbed out of the Land Rover. The towering black wall was behind them, receding quickly, looking for new victims to blind and harass.

'Well, thank God that's over,' she said with heartfelt relief, then she looked at him and burst out laughing. 'You should see your face! It's——' Suddenly she stopped and looked at herself in the wing-mirror. Oh, no! She too was covered in dust, her eyes staring out of a face like a clown's mask.

Kassim fetched one of the water-containers from the back of the vehicle and they used it to clean themselves up, then, as she brushed the sand from the windscreen, he checked the engine. At last, when they were ready to move, he started the engine, but as he began to turn the steering-wheel she placed her hand over his and said quietly, 'I've changed my mind, Kassim. We've come this far, so we may as well carry on and meet your friends.'

He looked at her without expression. 'So? Suddenly you are willing to put your fate in my hands? You are willing to trust me with your life?'

It wasn't so much a question as an ultimatum, and she was well aware of the position she was putting herself in if she answered yes. Swallowing the lump in her throat, she nodded, and wondered if there was any other person alive on earth to whom she'd have given such a promise.

'Good. I am well-pleased,' he said gravely. 'You will never have cause to regret it.' He gunned the accelerator, then cautioned her with a grim smile. 'A piece of advice, Janene. Do not call them Arabs. They are Berbers.'

They continued their journey east into the empty wastes of the desert.

Kassim was the first to spot the oasis and, as he pointed, she stared through the scratched windscreen. The rising waves of heat created strange shapes, but soon she made out the dark smudge on the horizon. As they drew nearer the smudge resolved itself into a substantial group of palm-trees. Scattered among them were large black tents.

Two figures atop camels began loping towards them, and Kassim grunted and halted the vehicle. As the riders rapidly approached, she saw the rifles slung from their shoulders and she looked nervously at Kassim. 'Who are they?'

'Camp guards,' he said casually. 'We'll stay here until they've identified me.'

It all sounded and looked a bit threatening to her but, before she could put her feelings into words, Kassim leaned over and gave her a hard yet sweet and lingering kiss. Then, with a soft command to stay in her seat, he got out and strode to the front of the Land Rover. Taking up a stance, his legs wide apart and his hands on his hips in a gesture of nonchalant command, he awaited the riders.

Her lips were still tingling and she hoped sincerely that it wouldn't turn out to be a farewell kiss. By the look of the two men who were now dismounting, it very well could be. Swathed in dark blue robes and black turbans, they had the fiercest-looking faces she'd ever seen. Glittering eyes over hooked noses and black pointed beards.

Suddenly they threw their arms wide in recognition, and an instant later they were both embracing Kassim like a long-lost brother. She heard the sound of loud laughter. There was more discussion and more laughter, then, with a final embrace, the two men remounted their camels and raced back to the oasis.

Kassim came into the Land Rover, settled himself in the driver's seat and grinned at her. 'We could follow them, but I'd rather wait, out of courtesy, to give them time to arrange their welcoming-committee. Ten minutes should be long enough.' He placed his hand innocently on the top of her thigh, feeling the flesh through the thin material of her robe. 'We'll have to think of some way of passing the time, Janene. Any suggestions?'

Removing his hand with the delicate use of her thumb and middle finger, she deposited it back on his own knee and said primly, 'I've no intention of passing it that way. Not here. Now, try and behave yourself.'

He heaved a sigh. 'There are no cold showers in the desert, alas. In this country a man's blood is always hot. Especially when he is in the presence of such alluring, delectable——'

'Why are they called the Blue Men?' she asked, cutting him off in mid-flight.

'An English trader put in at one of our ports many years ago. His cargo was indigo-dyed cotton. We Berbers were the first to trade with him, and we've been dressing in blue ever since.' He showed his strong white teeth in a hungry smile. 'But I'm sure we can find something much more interesting than that to talk about.'

His fingers were toying with her earlobe, sending

shivers down her back. 'There are unimaginable delights still in store for us,' he murmured seductively. 'New experiences. New heights of passion to be scaled. Would you like me to describe them to you now or would you rather wait in breathless anticipation?' Now his mouth was at her ear, his tongue doing things she'd never dreamed of.

She put her hand up to fend him off gently, but when he started nibbling at her fingers she pulled her hand away.

'Please, Kassim,' she implored shakily. 'You. . . You're making me uncomfortable.'

His blue eyes glinted wickedly. 'Uncomfortable? In what way?'

She swallowed and tried to think of something else. 'You know perfectly well what I mean. Now, stop it. If you must do something with your hands, pour me another drink.'

When Kassim judged that sufficient time had passed, he put the Land Rover in gear and headed for the oasis.

The reception-committee was lined up in readiness. About sixty men mounted on camels raised their rifles in the air and fired off a volley as Janene and Kassim stepped out of the Land Rover. Kassim raised his hand in greeting and spoke in Arabic.

She watched as the men dismounted and, as they strode purposefully towards them, she edged a little closer to Kassim and he muttered quietly, 'Hide your nervousness, little rose. No one is going to eat you. Put your head back and show them the fire and spirit in your eyes.'

In spite of his assurances, the next five minutes were the most nerve-racking she'd ever gone through. In complete silence the men filed slowly past, bowing respectfully to Kassim, then pausing before her for a brief yet penetrating scrutiny.

They were all tall and lean and held themselves with an almost regal dignity. Their faces, half masked by the ends of their turbans, were bronzed and their eyes the same brilliant blue as Kassim's. Their robes, in every shade of blue from cornflower to deep royal, were all lined in white cotton. A handsome yet scary bunch of ruffians, she decided.

With all those eyes staring at her, she felt like a rabbit in a den of lions, but, remembering Kassim's instructions, she stared right back at them in bold challenge.

Finally, the inspection over, they all squatted on the ground in a great circle beneath an enormous palm-tree. Kassim spoke to them briefly, then waited until a woman emerged from one of the tents. Dressed in black and with great almond eyes shining above her veil, she came over and took Janene by the arm.

'Go with her,' Kassim commanded sternly. 'Here, your place is with the other women, not the men.'

He was being infuriatingly patronising again, but she kept her temper in check and her mouth shut. Something in his eyes warned her that if she argued she'd live to regret it.

The woman led her towards the tent, smiling and chattering excitedly away in Arabic, but all Janene could do was smile in return and shake her head. 'Sorry. English? A little *Français*?'

The woman obviously didn't understand, but that did nothing to dampen her enthusiasm.

The tent was crowded with at least ten women and a

dozen assorted children, from babes in arms to boister-
ous five-year-olds. The walls of the tent were hung with
silk draperies. On the ground there were magnificent
hand-woven rugs and silk cushions. The whole place
was a blaze of colour—turquoise, gold, magenta, emerald-green. In contrast, all the women were dressed in
black, although they all wore so many heavy silver
chains and barbaric-looking necklaces that they seemed
to rattle as they moved.

Dishes of sweet cakes, biscuits and almonds were
offered, and glasses of fragrant mint tea were poured
from a huge silver teapot. If the men of the tribe had
seemed silent and reserved, the women made up for it,
and although Janene didn't understand a word they
were saying, she felt completely relaxed and happy.

The children soon overcame their shyness and gathered around her, and when she took one of the babies
into her arms the women nodded to each other in
approval.

It was about an hour later when Kassim came to
collect her. They said their farewells, then climbed into
the Land Rover and headed back west into the desert.

When the oasis was a long way behind them, Kassim
gave her an ironic smile. 'You see? You are pefectly
safe. I didn't sell you into slavery, as you feared.'

Tiredly she leaned her head on his shoulder. 'You
sound awfully pleased with yourself. I take it your visit
was a success? Honour and tradition fully satisfied?'

'Perfectly,' he said smoothly. 'They were quite
impressed with you.'

'Well, that's nice to know,' she murmured drily. 'Did
they tell you how much I was worth, then?'

It was meant to be a joke but his reply shook her

rigid. 'They assured me that I'd made a good trade-off. Their decision was that any man who'd let you go for such a price was a fool.'

She blinked, then sat up slowly and stared at him. 'Excuse me. I must have lost the place somewhere. What precisely are we talking about here? What do you mean by "trade-off" and "price"?'

'Fifty thousand pounds sterling,' he said blandly. 'That was the amount Damien owed my family. When I went over to England to collect it, he couldn't come up with the cash. Your ex-lover offered me you instead.' His right hand dropped from the wheel and caressed her thigh. 'The man is a fool, Janene. You're proving to be more of a bargain than I thought.'

For a moment she felt as if someone had just pushed her over the edge of a cliff, then she drew in her breath and said icily, 'Take your hand off my leg.'

Ignoring her, he gave her thigh a possessive squeeze, and in a blind rage she dug her nails into the back of his hand and scratched viciously, then yelled at him furiously, 'Touch me again and I'll scratch your eyes out.' She lunged for the ignition and switched it off, then, even as the Land Rover was skidding to a halt, she opened the door and jumped out.

## CHAPTER SEVEN

SHE'D walked about a hundred yards when the Land Rover drew up alongside her. He leaned from the driver's window and called, 'Get back in here, you foolish Englishwoman. This isn't the place for a leisurely stroll. It isn't Hyde Park. It's dangerous.'

Ignoring him, Janene hitched her robe higher and ploughed ahead with grim determination. Damn all men. . .and him in particular.

He kept pace with her, and from the corner of her eye she saw him thump the steering-wheel in annoyance. 'There are snakes and scorpions out there,' he shouted.

'Good,' she yelled back. 'It'll be an improvement on your company.' She squinted her eyes against the glare of the sun and pulled her headscarf lower over her face.

'You'll get heatstroke,' he warned. 'It's over a hundred degrees out there.'

'Go away! Leave me alone!' she shouted. 'I hate you. I never want to see you again. Never.'

He shook his head and looked imploringly at the sky. 'Allah, spare me from the peverse machinations of a woman's mind. Tell me, your humble servant, how I have offended her.'

'If you had a grain of decency in your body, you wouldn't have to ask a stupid question like that,' she cried. 'But you're just a big, unfeeling brute.'

He drove ahead for about two hundred yards, then

waited for her to catch up. 'You'll die of thirst,' he called as she drew level. 'That beautiful little body will be nothing but a heap of bleached bones.'

Her thin *babouches* weren't much protection and the soles of her feet were getting hot from the burning sand. She quickened her pace and he put the Land Rover in gear and kept alongside her.

'I've a good mind just to leave you here and teach you a lesson,' he growled through the open window. 'In this country, only mules are allowed to be stubborn. Women are supposed to do as they are told.'

'Leave me, then! I don't give a damn what you do. I told you that I never wanted to see you again, didn't I?'

He eyed her in amused exasperation, then complained, 'I can't leave you here to rot. I haven't had my money's worth yet.'

Almost exploding with rage, she picked up a stone and hurled it at him.

'You should take better aim,' he observed mildly. 'Anyway, it would be wiser to save your energy. You're going to need it.'

Sweat was trickling into her eyes, causing them to smart, and she drew her sleeve across her brow.

'Would you like a drink?' he asked politely. 'A large mug of cold, refreshing water?'

She didn't answer, because it was becoming too much of an effort and it just made her mouth drier.

Her feet were really burning now, but she wasn't going to give in. She'd crawl on her hands and knees if necessary.

'You're doing fine,' he called to her ironically about ten minutes later. 'You've walked a kilometre. Only another ninety-six to go.'

She blotted the sound of his sarcasm out and wiped her brow again. Walking on sand was hard on the leg-muscles, and hers seemed to be on fire. She stopped a moment for a rest, and he immediately challenged her, 'Had enough?'

Glaring at him, she took a deep breath and continued walking in silence.

'Two kilometres,' he shouted half an hour later. 'Ninety-five left.'

Her head was drooping with fatigue. If she could only sit down for five minutes. Then again, perhaps that wouldn't be a good idea. She might not be able to get up again. Doggedly she headed west.

'Are you sure you aren't going round in circles?' he mocked. 'People tend to do that in the desert. Don't rely on me. I'm following you.'

For a moment panic had her in its grip, then her mind cleared. He was just trying to scare her. As long as she kept that blasted sun in front of her, she was going in the right direction. Her eyes closed once more in fatigue, then jerked open as he gave a series of blasts on the horn.

He grinned at her and pointed to the sky. 'Vultures. I was scaring them off.'

It was only her anger that was sustaining her now. The man was a cold-hearted sadist. To think that she'd actually imagined that she was falling in love with him. . .

'Four kilometres.'

The voice seemed to come from a long distance and it took her a moment to get her mind in focus. Where was she. . .? Oh, yes. . . God, she was tired. . .and hot. . .and choking with thirst. Suddenly, with a groan of despair, she sank to her knees, her legs too weak to support her any more. The sand was burning the palms of her hands, but she was too exhausted to care.

A shadow fell cross her, and through blurry eyes she saw Kassim standing over her. 'All right, you magnificent, red-headed maniac,' he said softly. 'You've made your point. It's time to go home now.'

Bending down, he lifted her effortlessly into his arms, and with great tenderness carried her over to the Land Rover and lowered her into the passenger seat.

'Take this,' he ordered, handing her the mug. 'Don't gulp it. Sip it slowly.'

The cool water trickling down her parched throat was the sweetest thing she'd ever tasted. When the mug was empty she handed it back to him and said hoarsely, 'More.'

He refilled the mug. 'You're a fool,' he said amiably. 'An impetuous, glorious little fool. Did you honestly think you could walk all the way through the desert back to town?'

She eyed him with sullen resentment and he grinned. 'No. Of course you didn't. You're far too intelligent. But that temper of yours will be your undoing. I knew that you'd be upset when you learnt of the way Damien had betrayed you, but I didn't expect you to take off like an unguided missile.'

Janene finished the drink and resisted the urge to bounce the heavy mug off his thick skull. He'd torn a piece of white cotton lining from his robe and soaked it in cold water. She allowed him to tie it round her forehead, then she said bitterly, 'I was starting to like you. I thought you were a decent, civilised gentleman. I should have known better.'

He contrived an expression of injured pride. 'But I am civilised! And although I never had the benefits of an English public-school education, nor a chance to play cricket, I've always been considered a decent sort of chap.'

'Oh, yes. . .' she said with biting sarcasm. 'It was very decent of you to take me in lieu of the money you were owed. I hope you gave him a receipt.'

He shrugged. 'It was Damien's idea. Not mine.'

'It makes no bloody difference!' she fumed. 'You accepted the proposition and that makes you as bad as him. I'm a woman! A person! A human being! I'm not a damned animal in a livestock sale! Neither of you gave a damn about what my feelings might have been. I didn't count.' She paused, and would have curled her lip if it hadn't been so stiff. 'I'm sorry you haven't had your money's worth yet, but you've had all you're getting from me.'

He sighed and nodded in understanding, then appealed once again to heaven. 'My little rose feels slighted. That is understandable, but truly, the heat has addled her brains. Rather than punish me for my imagined sins, she punishes herself. But then, the English are well-known for their eccentricity, are they not? Now, if she were only to ask me why I agreed to her ex-lover's proposition, she'd prostrate herself at my feet and thank me for saving her from a fate worse than death.'

What the devil was he babbling about now? she wondered. 'Look. . .' she said tiredly. 'You're giving me a headache. Would it be asking too much to get this thing moving?'

He looked at her closely, and this time there was

genuine concern on his face. He fastened her seatbelt, looked into her half-dazed eyes again, then cursed himself softly under his breath and put the vehicle in gear.

Her headache gradually grew worse and she slumped down in her seat. She began to feel sick and giddy, then suddenly the darkness closed in on her.

When she came round she was lying in bed, covered with a cool silk sheet. The shutters were closed and, although the room was in semi-darkness, she could see the two figures conversing quietly over by the door. Her nausea had gone, but she was parched. As she attempted to sit up the pain lanced through her head, and with a groan she fell weakly back on to the pillow. When she opened her eyes again, Kassim and Sister Mary were standing over her.

'There, there,' said Mary, laying a hand on her brow. 'Just you lie there and don't be trying to get up for a while yet.' Glancing at Kassim she said, 'Her fever has gone.' Then, smiling down, she said. 'You'll be right as rain in no time at all.'

'Wh—what happened?' She sounded like a frog with laryngitis.

'You passed out,' Kassim told her grimly. 'Heat-stroke. It was my fault. May I be devoured by maggots. I should never have let you——'

'I need a drink,' she croaked. God! It felt as if something had died in her mouth.

Mary nodded sympathetically. 'Yes. That's the style. Drink as much as you can.' Looking at Kassim, she said quietly, 'I must be off now. I'll send Kebira up with a jug of iced lemon.'

As soon as they were alone, she looked up at Kassim and mumbled, 'I'm sorry. You did warn me. But I was too damned angry with you to listen.'

He sat down on the edge of the bed, facing her. 'Are you still angry?'

She looked up into those hard sapphire eyes and considered. 'Yes,' she said finally. 'I've every right to be, haven't I? Women are treated badly enough in this country without men like you thinking they can be bought like toys, to play with. As far as I'm concerned, you're just. . .' She paused, as it suddenly registered on her that beneath the sheet she was stark naked. Scowling up at him, she muttered, 'I suppose you had a good time undressing me?'

'Kebira undressed you and put you to bed,' he growled. 'I was preparing a salve for your feet.'

'Oh. . .' She could feel the bandages. 'I'm sorry. That was a tasteless thing to say.'

'It was,' he agreed. 'But you're forgiven. Now, as your physician, I order you to stay in bed. Tomorrow we'll take the bandages off and, hopefully, the blisters will have gone.'

He laid the palm of his hand on her brow, nodded in satisfaction, then gently lifted her wrist and felt her pulse. He gave a slight frown, looked into her eyes, and murmured, 'A little rapid, but nothing to worry about.'

Well, it would be rapid, wouldn't it? she thought. Every time he touched her the damn thing went into overdrive.

'I'll give you a couple of sleeping-pills,' he decided. 'A good night's rest is what you need.'

She shook her head. 'I've never taken a sleeping-pill in my life and I don't intend starting.' She eyed him caustically. 'I'll just imagine that I'm counting pound notes. Fifty thousand is a nice round figure. I should drop off by then.'

Kebira came in, bearing a jug and a glass on a silver tray. At a nod from Kassim she laid it by the side of the bed, then quickly withdrew.

Kassim filled the glass, then with his left hand supporting her shoulders, he helped her to sit up. Clutching the sheet modestly to her bosom with both hands, she sipped greedily as he held the glass to her lips.

'Slowly,' he warned. 'Your whole system has been overheated and it must be allowed to cool slowly.'

He sat with her patiently until she'd drained the glass, then he gently lowered her and got to his feet. 'Do you wish me to stay, or would you rather be alone? Some soothing music on the radio, perhaps?'

For some ridiculous reason she found herself wanting him to stay. 'Please yourself what you do,' she said indifferently, 'I couldn't care less.'

He sat down again on the edge of the bed and grinned. 'Good. In that case, I'll stay. Although you try to hide it, there is a look of loneliness in those beautiful eyes. A silent appeal no man could ignore.'

She scowled at him again. 'It isn't loneliness. It's boredom.'

'Very well,' he said generously. 'I shall do my best to unbore you. What shall we talk about?'

She had an insane urge to slap his face, then smother it with kisses. He was impossible. How could a man be so infuriating at one moment, then full of tender loving care the next? Did he really care for her that much, or was he merely looking after his investment?

'Let's talk about this deal you made with Damien,' she challenged.

He sighed. 'It's water under the bridge. I'd rather forget about it. And so should you.'

Oh, no! He wasn't getting off as easily as that. 'You realise that if I'd known about it sooner I'd never have gone to bed with you,' she said accusingly.

He smiled, a little too confidently for her liking. 'Are you sure about that, Janene? Sexual attraction is a force that should not be underestimated. You'd have talked yourself into it sooner or later.'

God! He was so damned sure of himself. Then again, she had a sneaking suspicion that he was right. He seemed to know more about the way her mind worked than she did herself.

It was time to get down to brass tacks, and she looked at him keenly. 'I always thought that Damien was good at his job. How did he end up owing you all that money?'

'It's a long story,' he warned.

'So? I'm not going anywhere. Doctor's orders. Remember?'

He sighed. 'I'd rather spare your feelings than go into all the sordid details.'

She narrowed her eyes at him. 'Never mind sparing my feelings. You can't make me feel any worse than you already have. I want to know how I ended up being haggled over and traded like a bag of potatoes.'

'There was no haggling, I assure you,' he said calmly.,

'No?' She raised a mocking brow. 'Is fifty thousand the going rate for a woman, these days? Even a second-hand one like me?'

He rose gracefully to his feet, tall, dignified, his face expressionless. 'I think it would be wiser if I left. In order to recover, you must rest and remain calm, but my presence here merely serves to stoke the fires of your anger.'

'Oh, sit down, you great muffin,' she said crossly. 'I'm perfectly calm. Anyway, I certainly won't rest until I know what happened.' She patted the side of the bed. 'Now, sit down and tell me the worst. I might claw your eyes out later, but for the moment you're in no danger.'

Kassim sat down, eyed her doubtfully for a moment, then gave a sigh of resignation. 'This all started because of a nephew of mine. His name is unimportant. Suffice to say that, until Damien got his hands on him, he was regarded as a credit to the family.' He paused and looked at her hopefully. 'Just tell me when you feel yourself getting bored, and I'll stop.'

'Please carry on,' she said quietly. 'You're doing fine.' She was going to find out the truth, even if he had to drag all his relatives in one by one.

'My nephew had been sent to study at the London School of Economics,' he went on grimly. 'Ironic, when you think of what subsequently took place. He was well provided for—a flat in Chelsea and enough money to cover his expenses for two years at least. Alas, he'd only been gone about six months when he wrote back to say that he was penniless and needed more cash. The boy's father is dead, so naturally his mother came to me and appealed for help. I ordered the boy home and demanded a full explanation.' He paused, and she saw his features hardening at the memory.

'I suppose this is where Damien comes in?' she sighed. 'Bad financial advice?'

He shook his head bitterly. 'There are good and bad financial advisers. Damien is neither. He is that foulest of all creatures, a jackal, who searches for meat for his masters and is content to live off their leavings.'

No one could put that amount of contempt into his voice unless he was absolutely sure of what he was talking about, she told herself.

'When my nephew confessed that he had lost the money gambling, I ordered certain of my associates in London to commence enquiries. It seems that your ex-lover is——'

'Stop calling him that!' Janene snapped in embarrassment. 'Ex-fiancé, if you must.'

'I bow to your wishes,' he growled. 'In future I will refer to him by name only. This creature, who calls himself Damien, has his fingers in many shady enterprises. According to my information, there is an illegal gambling-club in the festering bowels of Soho, where the drinks are doctored, the women distracting, and the card-dealers rejoice in such names as Six-Finger Jack and Weasel-Mouth Murphy. One of Damien's more lucrative sidelines is to introduce gullible and unsuspecting customers, tourists mostly, into this den of thieves. For this service, he receives ten per cent of the customers' losings. In the case of my nephew, Damien earned himself five thousand pounds.'

'Your nephew lost fifty thousand pounds in one night?' she asked in amazement.

'No. It was over a course of four nights. The first night he actually won eight hundred pounds, but that was just the bait to make sure he came back for the fleecing.'

She frowned. 'Well, he certainly pulled the wool over

my eyes. I was with Damien for six months, but I never suspected that he was into things like that.'

'Charm, Janene,' he observed bitterly. 'His stock-in-trade. And he had you.'

'Me?' she said indignantly. 'I had nothing to do with it!'

'Of course you didn't,' he said, soothing her ruffled feathers. 'But he needed a girl like you. Not just a beautiful face but an honest face. You were the perfect cover for his nefarious schemes. Most of his under-handed dealings were done in the anonymity of a crowd. You were his blind, unsuspecting partner.'

God! What a fool she'd been. Now that she knew the truth, it explained a lot. His sudden disappearance at parties to discuss 'business'. Some of the shifty-eyed characters she'd noticed him talking to.

She looked at Kassim sharply. 'So that's why you came to London. To confront him and get the money back?'

He shrugged. 'It was my duty. Apart from a need for revenge, the good name and reputation of my family were at stake. Anyway, I ran him to ground at the party. He was quite willing to pay back the money he'd made as commission, but that wasn't good enough. I told him as pleasantly as I could that I was holding him personally responsible for the full amount, and that if the full amount wasn't forthcoming he'd most certainly never be able to father any children.'

She suppressed a shudder. It seemed just the kind of threat that Kassim was capable of making and carrying out.

'It was then that he offered me you instead,' he informed her, with the hint of a smile.

That was still a bit hard to swallow, and her scepticism must have shown on her face, because he continued, 'The truth is that he offered you as security to hold until such time as he could raise the money.'

'Security?' The idea was so ridiculous that she almost laughed.

'Yes,' he drawled. 'I too thought it was an outlandish idea. After all, that's not quite the way one expects an Englishman to behave, is it? They usually leave that sort of thing to filthy foreigners like me, who don't know any better.'

'But you obviously took him up on the idea, didn't you?' she challenged.

Kassim didn't deny it, but went on to explain, 'After I'd got over my initial shock, I'll admit that I became intrigued. I'd already heard about you from my associates, who'd told me that——'

'You mean you had people spying on me?' she spluttered in indignation.

Unperturbed by the interruption, he continued, 'Told me that you were quiet and reserved and extremely attractive. When Damien pointed you out to me across the room, I could see that the description didn't do you justice. You weren't attractive. You were positively magnetic. I couldn't take my eyes off you.' He smiled wryly in recollection. 'Damien, the jackal, sensed my interest and suggested that I go and talk with you. Inspect the merchandise, in other words.'

She nodded grimly. 'I remember it well. "Let's step outside. It's much quieter on the balcony", you said. I suppose you intended to examine me at closer quarters. . .in intimate detail?'

He smiled again. 'As I recall, you protested. But not too vigorously.'

'At the time, I was under the impression that you were a friend of Damien's,' she retorted stiffly. 'Otherwise I might have slapped your face for taking liberties.'

'That would merely have heightened the desire that was already stirring in my loins,' he murmured.

She could see that desire in his eyes right now as he hovered over her, and she felt vulnerable under the thin silken sheet. Whatever he had in mind was abandoned with a sigh of regret and a look of self-reproach.

'After you left the party I told your ex—the jackal that I'd agree to his proposition, with one proviso. I'd forget about the money if he'd agree to co-operate in your abduction. He jumped at the chance like a rat at a piece of cheese, as I'd suspected he would. He said that he could arrange for you to be alone at a secluded cottage in Kent.'

At her look of disdain, he held up a hand to silence her and went on, 'I make no apoligies for what I did. The reasons seemed good enough at the time.'

'What reasons?' she asked in a curiously subdued voice. 'It seems a complicated and expensive way of satisfying your lust for a complete stranger.'

'Well, I'll admit that the prospect of making love to you was a major consideration, but there were others,' he drawled. 'I had gone to London to humiliate and take my revenge on the man who'd cheated my kinsman. What better way to humiliate him than return in triumph with the woman who was to be his wife?'

'Oh, I see,' she said drily. 'I was just the spoils of war. A trophy for the conquering hero?'

'A trophy worth her weight in diamonds,' he assured her.

His compliment did nothing to banish her vague feeling of—of what? Disappointment?

'You said there were other reasons,' she remarked coolly.

He remained silent for a moment, as if contemplating some great problem, then he shrugged. 'Let's just say that I felt sorry for you. At the time, you seemed hell-bent on marrying him. I couldn't stand by and see you throw yourself away on a wretched cur like him.'

'That was very considerate of you,' she said wood-enly. 'The gallant knight to the rescue. I suppose you'd have done the same for any woman. Well, you've had your reward, as far as I'm concerned. And since I no longer intend to marry Damien, you have no reason to keep me here.'

That put an abrupt end to the discussion. Even in the dim light she could see the tightening of his jaw-muscle and the hard set of his mouth as he got slowly to his feet. 'You need your rest, Janene,' he said quietly. 'Kebira shall sleep in this room tonight, should you require anything.'

She waited until he'd gone, then she clenched her fists and bit her lip. So he'd only felt sorry for her, had he? For a while she'd had this crazy idea that he might have. . . But no. He'd just felt sorry for her!

She stared miserably up at the ceiling and made her decision. Tomorrow she'd demand to be taken home as soon as possible.

# CHAPTER EIGHT

IN THE morning it took her a few frustrating minutes of sign-language before she managed to convince Kebira that she didn't want breakfast in bed, and was in fact recovered enough to go downstairs.

Sitting on the edge of the bed, she removed the bandages and examined the soles of her feet. They were still red and angry-looking, but the blisters had gone. Placing them cautiously on the floor, she stood up and decided that the pain wasn't bad enough to keep her from walking. The pain in her heart was something else, however. It looked as if she was just going to have to learn to live with that from now on.

After a shower, she dressed, then picked her way gingerly down to the courtyard.

Kassim was drinking coffee at the poolside and, as she approached, he rose and greeted her politely, 'Good morning, Janene. I hope you slept well. Come closer and let me examine you.'

Tight-lipped, she stood in front of him while his electric-blue eyes gazed deeply into hers. 'Yes. . .' he announced in satisfaction. 'As clear and sparkling as ever. Now show me your feet.'

He got down on one knee and she obediently raised one foot at a time. When he stood up, he assisted her carefully into a chair and pronounced, 'They are healing well. I think we'll go to the beach today.'

She shook her head firmly. 'No, thank you. I'm not going near sand again. Never. Forget it.'

He poured her a glass of orange juice and fixed her with a look of admonition. 'You'll do as you're told, Janene. As your doctor, I'm prescribing the necessary treatment. You're going to swim. Seawater will hasten the healing process on your feet.'

She supposed that it was sound advice, but the state of her feet wasn't the foremost thing in her mind at the moment. Drinking her orange juice, she eyed him cautiously over the rim of the glass, then, deciding that it was better to get it over with as quickly as possible, she put down her glass and said quietly, 'I want to go back to England. I can't stay here as—as your guest forever. It's time I was getting on with my own life.'

It was hard to tell what was going through his mind as he contemplated her in silence, and she felt a lump come to her throat. At last she'd found the courage to make a direct challenge, and a part of her was wishing that she hadn't.

Finally he gave her the briefest of nods. 'I understand. It shall be arranged.'

There had been a faint glimmer of hope, but his answer plunged her world into darkness. She continued to look into his eyes, determined not to show the slightest flicker of emotion. She'd preserve her dignity if it killed her.

'Good,' she said lightly. 'May I ask when these arrangements can be made?'

He shrugged apologetically. 'Three days' time. It can't be done any sooner. The plane is undergoing a mandatory major overhaul at the moment.'

There was a note of regret in his voice that made her

wonder. Was he sorry that she was demanding to go home, or was he sorry about the three-day wait until he could get rid of her?

'Three days will do fine,' she said stiffly. 'It'll give me more time to get samples from the market.'

His dark brows rose in query. 'Samples?'

'The local craftwork,' she explained patiently. 'I told you that I used to run a chain of boutiques in London. I intend going back into business with my partner.' If he'd only said the right words, it could have been so different, but she kept that bitter thought to herself.

His blue eyes were regarding her shrewdly. 'Are you telling me that these boutiques could sell the artefacts made in the back-rooms of the souk?'

Glad of the chance to focus her mind on something other than their precarious and dubious relationship, she nodded. 'I'm certain of it. The jewellery, leather-work, embroidered scarves and caftans. There's a real ethnic quality and originality.' She nodded again. 'They should sell well in London.'

He raised his cup in salute and murmured, 'Then, may I wish you every success in your venture, Janene? If there is any way I can help, you merely have to ask.'

He really meant it, she thought. Was he having an attack of conscience?

'Well. . .' she went on, still finding it hard to keep the dark despair of disappointment from her voice. 'If the goods prove as popular as I think they will, I'll have to return here and organise a regular supply. I was thinking along the lines of starting up a workshop. Good working conditions and modern equipment. And the workers will earn more because I'll buy their products at twice the price they can get here.'

He poured her more orange juice while she gave her order for breakfast to a servant, then he sat back and eyed her thoughtfully. 'You'll need someone to supervise the workers while you're in London,' he pointed out. 'Someone you can rely on.'

'Kebira,' she said quickly. 'She knows a lot of the craftsmen and artists here. And she knows the kind of quality I'm looking for.'

He gave a nod of approval at her choice. 'You can have her. As for the workshop, leave that to me. I'll have one purpose-built.' Seeing her eyes widen, he said drily, 'Don't worry. I'm not trying to bulldoze my way into your business. I welcome any enterprise which benefits the people of my town. My lawyer will also attend to any necessary paperwork, such as permits or export licences.'

It was more than she could have dreamed of. His generosity was postively embarrassing, and she averted her eyes from that steady, penetrating gaze, then stammered, 'It—it's very kind of you, Kassim.'

'It's the least I can do, Janene,' he replied softly. 'I'm very fond of you. I'd like to see you succeeding.'

She still couldn't look at him. He was fond of her. That wasn't the word her heart longed to hear, but it was better than nothing. 'Thanks,' she murmured, swallowing painfully.

'I'll make things even easier for you,' he added. 'Whenever you do decide to come back, just phone our embassy in London. They'll contact me, and within six hours my plane will be standing by for you at Heathrow.'

\* \* \*

The beach was vast and deserted, mile upon mile of golden sand scoured clean by the tide. It was a sight straight out of a holiday brochure. The huge, white-topped rollers from the Atlantic, losing their impetus far offshore on the shelving bottom, came to rest gently on the shoreline. The fierce heat of the sun was tempered by a cool, comfortable breeze.

After breakfast, Kebira had unearthed a skimpy two-piece swimming costume which she'd handed to Janene with a look of shocked outrage and a barely suppressed giggle. Janene had no intention of asking where it had come from or who it had belonged to.

She was wearing it now beneath loose trousers and a light cotton shirt. She watched Kassim through her sunglasses as he spread a large blanket on the sand. Next, he produced an enormous beach-umbrella from the rear of the Land Rover and positioned it over the blanket. He wasn't taking any chances of her catching heatstroke again.

Without wasting any time, he removed his robe. The tight white briefs looked startling against the dark, coppery hue of his body. Rather more sedately, she removed her shirt and trousers.

He ordered her to lie face-down on the blanket, then she squealed as something cold touched the nape of her neck. Squinting up at him, she gasped, 'What are you doing?'

'A complete sun-block,' he explained, showing her the bottle of oil. 'Beautiful women with red hair and creamy-white skin must take sensible precautions. Even while you're swimming, this will protect you.'

'Doctor's orders again?' she murmured.

His grin was slightly calculating. 'No. You are no

longer my patient. This is just friendly advice. Now, lie still and enjoy my tender ministrations.'

He began at her shoulders, his hands sliding sensuously over her smooth skin, and she bit her lip and closed her eyes and mentally recited all the stops on the London underground Central line. His strong fingers worked their way down, over her spine and on to her lower back and waist, and, when they finally insinuated themselves beneath the top of her briefs, she protested weakly, 'I don't need sun protection down there.'

He bent over and placed his mouth close to her ear. 'Better safe than sorry, Janene. They may inadvertently come off in the water.'

The backs and insides of her thighs were next to be treated, and by the time he'd finished her nerves were singing like taut harp-strings.

'Now turn over,' he said briskly.

She sat up and said in an unsteady voice, 'I—I'll do the front myself, if you don't mind.'

He handed her the lotion with a sigh of regret and a wry smile. 'Just as I was getting engrossed in my work. Would you snatch the bread from a hungry man's mouth?'

Again her tongue was getting dry, and the sight of that dark, hard body was playing havoc with her heartbeat. She tried her best to look calm and unruffled, but the tremble in her voice gave her away. 'Look. . .you go and have a swim. I'll come in when I'm ready.'

His laser-blue eyes mocked her gently. 'The sunblock is very important. I'd rather stay and make sure that you don't miss any parts.'

'I won't,' she assured him hastily. Her eyes lingered

for a moment on his tight briefs, then she looked away and said again, 'Get into the water. By the look of you, you need to cool off.'

He gave a throaty chuckle as he got to his feet. 'I doubt if there is enough water in all the oceans to cool my ardour for you, little rose.'

She watched as he waded out and dived into the water, and she bit her lip once again. Allowing herself to be brought to this deserted spot hadn't been one of her wiser moves, she thought with belated apprehension.

If Kassim tried to make love to her again, as he undoubtedly would, it would be hypocritical to refuse. It was a bit too late to start wearing a cloak of moral rectitude. In spite of her blighted hopes, he was still the same man as before. And if that sounded as if she was simply trying to find an excuse, so be it. Anyway, she knew her strengths and her weaknesses, and when it came to Kassim she was as weak as a kitten.

She removed her top and hurriedly applied the oil.

The sea was warm. She waded out until it was up to her waist, then she began swimming in long, lazy breaststroke. Feeling fresh and relaxed, she rolled on to her back, kicking her legs gently and moving her arms to keep afloat. Glancing sideways, she saw Kassim swimming strongly towards her. As he drew nearer, she saw his white teeth flash and heard him shout, 'Ahoy there, little English corvette! Surrender now and prepare to be boarded.'

Joining in the game, she shouted back, 'Never! I will fight to the death.' Then she turned on her stomach and struck out in a fast crawl for the shore. He caught up with her easily and, as his arm grabbed her round the waist, she stopped swimming and let her feet rest on the sandy bottom.

The water came up to her breasts, and he surveyed her with surprise. 'You've no top on!'

'Should I be wearing one?' she asked innocently.

'Yes,' he said in mock disappointment. 'You have deprived me of the pleasure of removing it.'

Just as long as he didn't think she was a lewd, brazen hussy, she told herself. 'I—I don't make a habit of swimming topless,' she said defensively. 'But the place is deserted and it—it's more comfortable.'

He nodded wisely, then gave a wide grin. 'I'm all for comfort. And the beauties of nature. You look like some delectable little sea-nymph standing there *au naturel*.'

The sun glistened on his dark skin, then suddenly everything was blotted out as his lips descended on hers and he crushed her against his chest. His kiss was urgent, almost desperate, his tongue exploring and ransacking the sweet depths of her mouth, and she responded with an equal hunger.

Suddenly releasing her, he drew in a great lungful of air before disappearing under the water. She felt his hands on her waist, then the slight tug as her briefs were removed. A moment later he surfaced and gave a reckless smile. 'There! Now we are both more comfortable.'

Once again he held her in a crushing embrace, and once again she swept all her doubts and misgivings into a neglected corner of her mind and abandoned herself to the dark forces of passion.

She clung to him fiercely, her arms reaching up and

entwined round his neck, her breasts taut against his chest and her lips feeding hungrily off his.

His hands slid slowly from her shoulder-blades downwards, and she felt herself being lifted buoyantly out of the water. In mute submission she gazed down into his hungry eyes, then he forced her legs apart with his knee and gently lowered her on to himself.

She buried her face against his shoulder to stifle her gasps, then she wrapped her legs round him and dug her fingers into the hard flesh of his back. Slowly and sensuously he began to lift and lower her, until, in a frenzy, she began urging him on.

In glorious union they reached the ultimate height of passion and in the violence of consummation she threw her head back and cried his name aloud. Slowly and sweetly the tension drained away, but she remained clamped to him like a limpet, accepting his tender and grateful kisses.

'I'm sure that did my feet a lot of good,' she murmured dreamily in his ear. 'I can feel the benefit already.'

He bit lightly at her neck, then gave a throaty chuckle. 'I must write a treatise some time on the therapeutic effects of lovemaking. We'll repeat the treatment a little later on and test the theory.'

'Yes,' she said thoughtfully. 'You can't write a treatise until you're sure of the facts.'

'And no one could have a more co-operative or delightful subject to experiment on,' he teased. Gently he untangled her, then, drawing in a deep lungful of air, he dived under the water and retrieved their briefs. She slipped hers on, then hand in hand they waded towards the shore, where she flopped exhaustedly on to the blanket.

Kassim lay beside her, propped up on one elbow and gazing down at her in admiration.

She opened one eye and quizzed him. 'What are you looking at?'

He grinned. 'Those lovely ripe breasts.'

She sat up and reached for her discarded top, but he restrained her. 'Don't. I like you the way you are.'

Lying down again, she smiled and scolded him lightly. 'You don't have to sit there like a guard-dog. They aren't going to run away. Go and do something useful, like bringing me something to eat. You did remember to bring food, I hope?'

He nodded. 'There's supposed to be a cool-box with chilled white wine and chicken in the back of the Land Rover. If there isn't, then I'll go back and suspend the chef by his thumbs over a hot fire.'

It was the kind of amusing remark he was always making, not meant to be taken seriously, and she replied in a similar vein, 'It was your idea to come here to the back of beyond, miles from the nearest restaurant. You should have checked before we left. If I get faint and collapse from hunger after all that exhausting "treatment", it's your fault and no one else's.'

The effect on him took her by surprise. For a moment his eyes seemed tortured, then he looked away and said quietly, 'You are perfectly right. A man who fails to provide for the comfort and security of his woman is not worthy of the name. All last night I wrestled with my conscience. I thought I had won, but your words have merely confirmed what I knew in my heart all along.'

She sat up slowly, looking at him in utter perplexity. 'Look. . .you don't have to make such a big deal out of it. I mean. . .I'm not sitting here starving to death. I didn't mean you to take me seriously. It—it was just a pretty rotten joke, that's all.'

Her words did nothing to alter the fierce scowl on his face, and he muttered darkly, 'It's no joke to me.'

Baffled by his behaviour, she could only stare at him in silence, then, taking things into her own hands, she struggled to her feet, marched over to the Land Rover and found the cool-box. Bringing it back, she thrust it into his hands. 'There! Now, will you stop being so moody and dramatic. You're spoiling the day.'

For a moment he remained remote and withdrawn, his eyes fixed unseeingly on the distant horizon, then he recovered and shrugged. 'Once again I am at fault. We have only a short time left to be together, but instead of enjoying every precious second I wallow in guilt and self-reproach.'

'Well, I'm not quite sure I know precisely what it is you feel guilty about,' she pointed out. 'But what's done can't be undone, so there's no point in worrying about it. You told me that yourself, didn't you? You told me that each day of your life was supposed to be a fresh page.'

His blue eyes studied her in surprise, then he nodded. 'There speaks the tongue of a wise woman. But a man must face the truth about his shortcomings or he is less than the dust at his feet.'

She frowned, getting more puzzled by the minute. 'I still don't understand. What shortcomings are you talking about?'

He dismissed the subject with a shrug. 'They are not

a matter for discussion.' He opened the cool-box and produced the bottle with a flourish. 'Life must go on, little rose. Let us enjoy each other's company while we can.'

He poured the wine and dished up the cold chicken on a plate, and for a while they were content to eat and drink in silence, immersed in their own thoughts.

Finally, after wiping his fingers on a napkin, he poured some more wine and announced his plans. 'When I take you home I intend staying on in London for a while.'

Although her heart skipped a beat, she managed to sound casual. 'It's a big place. I'm sure you'll find plenty to do.'

He sipped at his wine, then said quietly, 'I'd like you to show me over this business you intend rejoining. If it's as good as you say it is, I may invest some money. It would give you extra capital should you wish to expand your outlets, wouldn't it?'

She smiled at him drily. 'Now, why would a rich and powerful man like you be interested in a small chain of boutiques? I shouldn't have thought that was your style.'

'I have my reasons,' he drawled. 'Are you interested or not?'

'It isn't up to me,' she pointed out coolly. 'I'd have to see what Sally thinks about——'

He held up his hand. 'I'll deal with that obstacle when I come to it. At the moment, it's your reaction I'm interested in. Would you have any personal objections to taking me on as a partner? A silent partner, needless to say. I would never dream of interfering in the day-to-day running.'

Hedging for time until she could get her thoughts back together, she said. 'You'd be taking a risk.'

'I like taking risks,' he assured her, with a confident smile.

'Well. . .what sort of return would you be expecting on your investment?'

'I'd be happy with the current bank-rate.'

She chewed at her lip for a moment, turning over the implications in her mind. The cold, unfeeling logic of reason was telling her that it would be better to make a clean and final break with this man. The trouble was in getting her heart to listen. He was becoming too much of an addictive craving.

Seeing the doubt on her face, he went on softly, persuasively, 'Of course, even as a silent partner, it would be common business practice for me to come over occasionally to see how things are going.' He paused, then added even more softly, 'And it would give us a chance to keep up our friendship. I'd like that very much, Janene.'

Friendship? she thought bitterly. Who did he think he was fooling? Why didn't he just come out with it and tell her bluntly that he wanted to keep her as a lover but that that was as far as he was prepared to go?

Swallowing the bile in her throat, she eyed him with quiet determination. 'It doesn't sound like such a good idea to me, Kassim. I'd have to think about it very carefully.'

He accepted her decision with a sigh of resignation, as if it was no more than he'd expected, then she felt herself melting under the full, devastating power of his blue eyes. 'There are no strings attached to my offer,

Janene. I would never want you to do anything that you thought was wrong.'

'I—I said I'd think about it,' she said shakily.

'Good. I can ask for nothing more. . .' He drew closer and ran his forefinger lightly over her lips. 'Except for another taste of that sweet mouth.'

It was two days later when Janene made her final trip to the souk with Kebira. The plane would be ready the following morning, and this was her last opportunity to obtain samples to take back to London.

When Kebira had heard the news, she'd been inconsolable at the thought of losing her new mistress, and she'd looked at her with big, sad eyes and asked, '*Pourquoi*?'

'Why am I leaving?' Janene had echoed. 'Because there's nothing here for me, Kebira. If Kassim loved me, I'd stay. He'd only have to ask, but he won't.' She'd paused and smiled at the distraught face. 'You don't understand a word I'm saying, Kebira, but if I can just talk about it, maybe I can get him out of my system.'

The large, liquid eyes had looked at her soulfully and she had gone on, 'I don't really blame him. There was a time I didn't want to settle down. That was when I felt guilty about my parents. I think Kassim is much the same. He has a good, full life and he has no need for a wife yet. He isn't ready to commit himself and I'm not content just to be someone's mistress.' She sighed. 'Of course, I may be wrong. But it's the best I can come up with at the moment.'

Kebira, not understanding the words but aware of the general sentiment behind them, could only shake her head dolefully at a world in which happiness could be so transitory.

Janene had hugged her, then said brightly, 'But you have nothing to worry your pretty head about. You're still going to be working for me. You're going to be my right-hand woman in Morocco. Kassim has promised that I can have you. When everything is sorted out, I'm inviting you to London for a while. You'll meet Sally, visit our shops, and learn to speak English.'

Kebira simply stared at her, looking lost and bewildered.

When they reached the market, Janene confidently followed Kebira through the tortured maze of narrow alleys. This was a part of the souk she'd never visited before, but Kebira had assured her by sign-language that this was the place for good-quality leatherwork.

Since it was impossible to walk two abreast in the crowded alleys, she kept as close behind Kebira as possible. As before, the souk was a bedlam of noise, music and shouting, and good-natured argument. The people, women with babies clinging to their backs mostly, and in every shade from the light browns of the Arabs to the rich ebony of the Africans, were friendly enough, although she couldn't fail to notice the occasional look of hard suspicion reserved for infidels and foreigners.

Ahead of her Kebira was beckoning from a doorway, and carefully she edged past a vendor who was squatting on the ground with a display of spices on a board.

The room she found herself in was cramped but well lit by oil-lamps. An old man crouching over a workbench straightened up and bowed politely to his visitors. Kebira spoke to him quietly, explaining what they were wanting, and with a nod of understanding he began to cover the bench with samples of his work—leather belts, waistcoats and slippers.

Impressed by the butter-softness of the leather and the quality of the work, Janene bought a selection of his goods, then gave instructions that they were to be delivered to Kassim's house that evening.

They left the house and wandered further into the depths of the souk, and it was while she was inspecting the shell necklaces at one of the stalls that she again had that peculiar feeling of being watched. Turning quickly, she surveyed the sea of faces behind her but everyone seemed preoccupied with their own business.

What was wrong with her? she wondered. She'd never been the nervous type but she'd had the same feeling the last time she'd been here. Casting a final suspicious eye over the crowd, she dismissed her feelings but kept a tight hold of her money as she followed Kebira.

They wandered into another alley and inspected some more stalls, and still the back of her neck had that cold, apprehensive prickle of fear. Afraid of making a fool of herself in front of Kebira, she kept her mouth shut. After all, it could be nothing more than her own over-active imagination playing tricks on her.

But it wasn't imagination, after all. . .

She was walking past one of the innumerable dark and forbidding openings between the stalls, and Kebira was only a few steps ahead, when the man grabbed her from behind. One arm encircled her waist, lifting her clear off the ground, and the other hand clamped itself sweatily over her mouth, cutting off her squeal of alarm. In her last sight of daylight she saw Kebira strolling unsuspectingly on, and then she was dragged into the darkness and some sort of evil-smelling sack was thrown over her head.

Her assailant released her and she instinctively reached up to remove the sack, but a guttural voice snapped at her and she was prodded forward.

Near to the edge of panic, she could feel a scream building up in her throat, but she summoned her courage and kept quiet. No one would hear a scream and it might only serve to anger her attacker, whoever he was.

He kept prodding at her back viciously, so that she stumbled forward, bouncing off the walls of what was obviously a narrow corridor. Occasionally she was guided to the right or left, and once she banged her head on a low entrance, but there was no let-up as she was driven relentlessly onwards.

Whoever was taking liberties with her was going to be in big trouble when Kassim heard about this, she told herself. If this was some crazy robber after her money, he'd be better to take it now and run, before she could get a good look at him.

The smell of the sack over her head was making her feel sick, but it was impossible to hold her breath for long. It was also impossible to keep track in her mind of all the twists and turns they'd been making, and she only hoped she could find her way out of this rabbit-warren when this was over.

After what seemed like an eternity of stumbling around passageways, she was half dragged down a stairway. She heard the creak of a door, then it slammed shut behind her and the sack was pulled from her head.

# CHAPTER NINE

BLINKING her eyes in the sudden light, Janene only had a moment to glimpse her surroundings before another shove in the back sent her sprawling to the floor. For a moment she remained on her hands and knees, gasping, her throat clogged with fear, then she raised her head and looked around her in amazement.

Decadent opulence were the words that sprang to mind. A sickening, marzipany luxury. There was a vast bed with a carved ivory headboard and black silk sheets. It was overhung by a canopy of purple silk. Red and gold striped cushions were scattered all over the deep-piled carpets. A cloying smell of perfume filled the air. And there were bronze statues. She looked at a couple of them, then turned her head away in disgust. And the paintings were just as bad. It didn't test the imagination too much to know what went on in this room.

Almost shaking with a potent mixture of anger and fear, she struggled to her feet and glared at her attacker.

He was standing in front of the closed door, legs wide apart and arms folded across his chest, barring her exit. Tall and brutishly strong, wearing a black robe and a dirty turban, he had a hooked nose, a rat-trap mouth and a deep scar down one cheek.

Inwardly quaking with terror, she adopted an

expression of outrage and marched over to confront him. 'Get out of my way! I'm leaving here right now.'

He gazed down at her impassively through slitted eyes, then suddenly he snarled threateningly in Arabic.

She backed away from him and looked around the room in desperation. This was getting to be a habit. Snatched from her cottage in Kent, and now snatched in broad daylight from a market in Morocco! Kassim had been responsible for the first, but whose idea was this? Obviously, that great ruffian at the door was only carrying out someone's orders. He didn't look as if he had the brains to put his own shoes on. So who was he working for? And why had they picked on her?

Realising that her only hope lay in bluffing her way out of this situation, she drew herself erect, trying to look as regal and formidable as possible, and said icily, 'I don't think you realise who you're dealing with here. I demand to be set free immediately or it'll be the worse for you.'

He snarled at her again in Arabic and her heart sank. If he didn't understand English, there wasn't much use in trying to threaten him. Thinking furiously, she stared at him in frustrated anger, then shouted, 'Kassim Riffik! You've heard of Kassim Riffik, haven't you?'

The slitted eyes opened for an instant. It wasn't much of a reaction but it was enough, and she shouted at him again, 'Kassim Riffik!' Then she pointed to herself. 'I belong to him. Do you understand, you ugly great ape? Kassim will tear your tongue out and feed it to the dogs.'

'Kassim Riffik will do nothing,' grated a voice behind her.

She turned quickly and saw the curtain fluttering at a

concealed entrance by the bed. The man who'd just stepped through and spoken was short and squat, with thick rubbery lips and protuding eyes. She recognised him immediately and searched her memory for his name. Hassan! The man who'd divorced his three wives. 'You!' she uttered. 'Are you responsible for this?'

The globular eyes leered at her and bowed in mockery. 'I see you recognise me, Miss Peters.' At her look of surprise, he said smugly, 'Yes. I have found out all about you, Englishwoman. Your name. Where you come from, and why you are in Morocco.' He looked past her and growled an order at the guard, who left the room.

Hassan eyed her again, then his thick lips parted in an evil grin. 'He is standing outside, so a sudden dash for freedom will avail you nothing.'

'All right,' she said acidly. 'I don't know what game you think you're playing, but you'd better get your hired thug to lead me out of here. I've no doubt that the girl who was with me is already raising the alarm. When Kassim gets here, he'll——'

'As I already said, he can do nothing,' scoffed Hassan. 'He will search for you but he'll never find you.' He made a sweeping gesture with his hand. 'This room, this apartment—very few people know of its existence. Only one or two of my most trusted friends. This is going to be your home for the next two years, Miss Peters. I suggest that you start getting used to the idea.'

She looked at him in open-mouthed astonishment, then she laughed derisively. 'You're mad! Insane! You can't keep me here.' His face darkened with anger, and as he stepped nearer she warned him sharply, 'Don't come any closer.'

He took another step, then stopped, and the anger on his face turned to cunning. 'Don't worry. I'm not going to harm you. It would be foolish to damage the merchandise.' He lit a thin, foul-smelling cigar and contemplated her with amusement. 'I've no doubt that you are burning with curiosity. You'd like to know why you have been brought here and what fate has in store for you. However, that can wait for the moment. First, I'd like to show you over my secret little love-nest. I'm quite pleased with it.'

Love-nest? She barely repressed a shudder as she glared at him. 'Don't start getting any ideas about me, you—you reptile,' she said tremulously. 'I'd sooner die that let you. . .' She started a fit of coughing as he blew a stream of strong cigar-smoke into her face.

'How very English,' he sneered. 'Death before dishonour. A ridiculous satement when one remembers that survival is the strongest of all the human instincts.'

Still racked by a fit of coughing, she suddenly felt her wrist being grabbed and she was almost yanked off her feet. Off-balance, she couldn't prevent herself being pulled towards the bed.

Desperately she clawed at the hand round her wrist, trying to pry his fingers loose, and hoping she'd break a couple of them in the process. He gave a powerful heave and let her go, and she went flying through the curtained entrance in the wall by the bed. On her hands and knees again, she looked up with pain-filled eyes as he stood over her, his face glistening with sweat.

'Get up, you infidel bitch,' he snarled.

'By God, you're going to pay for this,' Janene

promise him breathlessly. Getting slowly to her feet, she glanced around. This room was smaller than the other. There was a comfortable settee, a dining-table, a bookcase. It was sparsely furnished but clean, with tiled floor and walls and, thankfully, none of those horrible statues. There were two heavy doors set in the far wall, and he pointed to the first. 'Through there is the bathroom. The other door leads to the kitchen and is kept locked. You are not permitted to go in there.' He went over to it and pressed a button set in the wall. Almost immediately she heard the sound of a heavy bolt being withdrawn on the other side. The door swung open and an ancient crone, stooped and wearing a black shawl, shuffled through with a tray. Without uttering a word or looking at either of them, she laid the tray on the table, then shuffled out again. The door closed behind her and the heavy bolt shot home again.

'That was Fatima,' Hassan said, flicking his cigar-ash on the floor. 'She will bring you your food and anything else you may require. Simply press the bell when you want to summon her. As you can see, she has already brought you coffee.'

'It's probably drugged,' Janene muttered in accusation.

He poured some into a cup and handed it to her with a smile of mockery. 'Why should I waste money on drugs? Hunger and thirst will make you just as compliant to my wishes.'

She took the cup from him, then hurled the contents at his face. He managed to step sideways in time, and lashed his palm across her cheek.

Yet again she found herself on the floor. This time her ears were ringing and her jaw ached. His bulbous eyes were murderous, and he snarled, 'Try my patience any further and I'll take a whip to you. A few cuts on your back won't worry my friends. At least it will show them that your fangs have been drawn.'

Shakily she got to her feet and eyed him uneasily. He had friends? This was getting worse by the second, if that was possible. 'You're pretty tough with women, aren't you?' she taunted. 'The last time I saw you, in Kassim's courtyard, you were trembling in your shoes.'

His face darkened at the memory. 'That Berber pig humiliated me, but Allah has now provided me with the means of revenge.'

'It isn't Kassim's fault that you aren't man enough to father any children,' she snapped, driven by her anger to utter the biggest insult she could think of. 'If you had treated your wives decently, you wouldn't have been taken before him.'

'Close your mouth, woman!' he shouted at her. 'You are a stranger. You know nothing of our centuries-old customs.'

She glared at him in stony silence. There was no doubt that he was a mean, vicious, evil-minded thug, and a man like that could only be pushed so far. He'd already slapped her once. Next time he might go further.

He chewed on his cigar, letting his rage subside, then the look of sly cunning returned to his oily face. 'Over the years, Kassim Riffik has made many powerful enemies. I know them all. Men from the cities and the desert tribes. Already my messengers are contacting them, inviting them here. Can you imagine the pleasure they will get at the thought of violating the woman of their worst enemy?'

He cackled at his own cleverness. 'Ah, the beauty of such a scheme. That spawn of Shaitan sought to ruin me. But as he searches in vain for his lost love, my friends will be paying me very well to be entertained by her in this little love-nest. In two years' time I will have been repaid twice over. By then, unfortunately, you will be too hard-worn to command such a high fee, but you will be smuggled to a friend of mine in Egypt. The clients in his establishment are not so fastidious.'

She could almost feel the blood freezing in her veins. People read about things like this happening but, even in their worst nightmares, never imagined that they would be victims. She'd have to think of something. Anything!

Hassan had been watching the play of emotions on her face with sly amusement, and he blew another cloud of cigar-smoke in her direction. 'Kassim Riffik will have to look elsewhere for a bride. Perhaps I should arrange to have her stolen as well. Then you will have someone to share your sorrow with and I shall become even richer.'

Her eyes widened in surprise, then she said contemptuously, 'You're madder than I thought, Hassan. You should have got your facts right. Kassim has no intention of marrying me. If your spies had done their job right, they'd have told you that Kassim is taking me back to London tomorrow morning.'

'Still your lying tongue, woman,' he jeered. 'He took you to the Blue Men, didn't he?'

She shrugged, wondering what he was driving at. 'That's right. It was just a social visit. So what?'

'I told you that you were ignorant of the customs here,' he said with a smile of mockery. 'It is a tradition in his tribe that, if the chief desires a woman to be his wife, she must be presented before them for their approval. Especially so if she is an infidel.'

Her mouth worked silently for a few moments, then she swallowed. 'I—I don't believe you. He—he would have said something to me.'

He shrugged. 'Whether you choose to believe or not is no concern of mine.' He walked over and pressed the buzzer by the door, and as it opened to let him out he laughed at her in derision. 'The first of your clients should be here by tomorrow. Make sure you give him his money's worth or I'll have you screaming for mercy. Until then, I will leave you with your thoughts.'

She heard the bolt slam home, locking her in, then there was absolute silence and she looked around her prison in despair.

This was madness. Kassim would surely find her. Someone on the outside had to know about this place.

On the other hand, Hassan was as cunning as a fox and, like a fox's, his lair would be well hidden. She remembered stumbling down some steps. For all she knew, this place could be twenty feet under the ground. But someone had to find her! The alternative was too horrendous to contemplate.

God! She felt like sitting down and weeping, but an ocean of tears wasn't going to solve this problem. If she couldn't rely on outside help, she'd have to do it herself. Surely there must be some way to escape.

She looked around the room again. There were no windows, so how did the fresh air circulate? Searching carefully, she found a narrow grille at the foot of one of the walls. Lying down, she pressed her ear against it and heard a faint, distant hum and felt a gentle stream of cool air on her cheek.

Well, that was how the fresh air got in. How did the stale air get out? Heat rises. She glanced up, saw the grille in the ceiling, and gave herself ten Brownie points.

Dragging one of the chairs over, she climbed up and, by standing on tiptoe, she could touch the grille and no more. So, that was out of the question. If this had been a film, she'd have managed to take the screws out with a nail-file, remove the grille and crawl through the ducting to safety. But this was real life. She didn't have a nail-file and, even if she had, the damned opening was far too small.

Going through to the bedroom, Janene studied the door through which she'd been so unceremoniously pushed. Knowing that it would be a waste of time, she nevertheless tried the handle. No use. And the grille in the ceiling here was the same size as the other.

Refusing to give up hope, she returned to the other room. Pushing open the bathroom door, she glanced inside. Lavatory, bath, shower, all in gleaming pink porcelain. Coloured bottles of oils and lotions on a shelf.

That left the door leading to the kitchen. There had to be another exit from this place through there, and there was only one way to find out. She pressed the buzzer on the wall.

Nothing happened. She pressed again impatiently. Her plan was born of desperation and depended on whether Hassan had left the apartment or not. It might work or it might not, but at least she had to try.

At last she heard the sound of the bolt being withdrawn, and as soon as the door began to open she curled her fingers round the edge and wrenched at it with all her might. Taking the old woman by surprise, she dashed past her, then skidded to a halt in the middle of the kitchen and groaned in despair.

Hassan rose from the table, his face dark with fury. She backed away, but not before she'd had time to note the layout of the place. The door she was looking for was at the far end of the kitchen, a heavy-looking affair with iron studs. But worst of all it was guarded by another of his thugs.

'I warned you not to come in here,' Hassan snarled. 'Perhaps a few days shackled to the bed will teach you obedience.'

Choking back her anger, she retreated through the door before he decided to turn his threat into reality.

The bolt slid home again with a sound of dull finality, and she bit at her lip in frustration. Taut with nerves, she began restlessly pacing around the room. The icy fingers of panic were starting to reach into her mind, and she shuddered.

She looked at her watch. Only an hour had passed since she'd been dragged here. It seemed more like a year. She'd be a gibbering idiot soon if she didn't pull herself together.

It was late into the evening when she heard the bolt in the door being withdrawn again. Keeping well back, she watched warily as the old woman shuffled in with another tray and took the first one away without a word.

She wasn't the least bit hungry. Fear and tension had robbed her of any appetite, yet she knew that she had to eat, if only to keep up her strength. Examining the tray, she found another jug of coffee and a large bowl of chicken and vegetables and something that looked like semolina. Without much enthusiasm she picked up the spoon and began to eat. She managed to get half of it down, then pushed the bowl aside and poured herself some coffee.

Much as it frightened her to admit it, it didn't look as if the cavalry was coming to her rescue. If Kassim did know about this place, he'd have been here by now. Since Hassan seemed to be about the only enemy he had in this town, he must surely have guessed that it was he who was behind her disappearance. Or perhaps he did know but he just didn't care. He might have decided that, as he no longer had any use for her, Hassan was welcome to her. At least it would save him the trouble of flying her back to England.

No! Dammit! She got to her feet, fists clenched in determination. She was starting to crack up already. She was playing right into Hassan's hands. He wanted to break her mind and her spirit—turn her into a vacant-eyed, submissive puppet for the amusement of his friends. He was quite right. Why waste money on drugs? Her own enervating terror would do the job just as well.

Instead of brooding about the fate he had in store for her, she had to keep her mind occupied with something else. Determinedly she walked over to the bookcase and took down one of the volumes. Opening it, she turned the pages with a feeling of revulsion. It was written in Arabic but the pictures needed no explanation. The next two books were the same.

Calmly she carried the lot of them over to the table, then she sat down and began methodically ripping the pages out one by one. Three hours later her fingers were bruised and aching, but the whole library of filth lay in shreds on the floor.

Eyeing her handiwork with satisfaction, she got to her feet. Hassan would probably have a fit when he saw what she'd done. With any luck, it would be fatal.

Nervous exhaustion finally began to take its toll and she could feel her eyelids drooping. She curled up on the settee, with her head on a cushion, and after a while slipped into an uneasy doze.

Dreams of dark foreboding slithered through her mind, and in her restless sleep she moaned and fidgeted. Then one dream, more vivid than the others, found her crouched in a corner while a crowd of men shouted and haggled over her. In the midst of them Hassan was snarling at her to stand up and remove her robe.

Hassan yelled again and her eyes jerked open. This was no dream! There was the most unholy racket and screams coming from the kitchen. Wide-eyed with fear, she leapt from the settee.

Suddenly the door burst open, and as the tall figure strode in she sobbed in relief and flew into his arms. 'Kassim. . .Kassim. I knew you'd come.'

'Hush, little rose,' he murmured in her ear as she trembled against him. 'You are safe now.'

Behind him, Hassan, slumped and grey with fear, stood flanked by two of the Blue Men she'd seen at the oasis.

'Have you been harmed in any way?' Kassim asked her quietly.

Too overcome with relief and emotion to speak, she could only shake her head.

He continued to look at her closely, examining every line and detail of her features. 'If he as much as laid one of his foul fingers on you, I want to know,' he insisted quietly.

She could guess at what he really wanted to know and she found her tongue. 'It—it's all right, Kassim. He didn't do anything like that. All he did was slap me on the face.'

His lips tightened and his blue eyes were filled with a glacial hatred as he turned to confront Hassan. 'You struck her,' he accused softly. 'You dared to raise your hand and strike her.'

The Arab's thick lips were quivering in terror. 'I swear that it was an accident, Caid. A slip of my hand. I didn't mean to. I swear by Allah.'

'Silence!' roared Kassim. 'Mention Allah's name again and I'll have your lips sewn together.'

He stood glaring with suppressed rage at the man for a moment longer, then he turned his back on him and examined the room. 'What's through there?' he asked.

'That's the—the bedroom,' she told him. 'It's revolting.'

Determined to see for himself, Kassim went through. Moments later he returned with a look of disgust on his face and he grabbed Hassan by the throat with one hand. 'This place will be destroyed. Erased from the face of the earth. As I should destroy you, you stinking heap of manure.' He snapped an order to one of the Blue Men, who instantly produced a rope which he tied round Hassan's neck.

The globular eyes looked ready to pop out, and Janene grabbed Kassim's arm and gasped, 'You—you aren't going to hang him, are you?'

He smiled at her grimly. 'He is a dog, and like a dog he is going to be kept on a lead. Later, he will probably wish that we had hanged him.' At a gesture from him, the Blue Men jerked at the rope, dragging Hassan after them.

Kassim took her hand in his, squeezed it gently, then said, 'Come, little rose. I will take you home.'

# CHAPTER TEN

THERE was no sign of Kassim when Janene went down for breakfast the following morning. Deciding not to wait, she ordered her usual breakfast. Whatever it was he'd made her drink last night had not only given her a good night's sleep but had restored her appetite.

She was wearing the same clothes she'd arrived in. Kebira had shaken her head sadly as she'd watched her mistress getting dressed, and had tried her best to persuade her to wear one of the gorgeous, multi-coloured robes. But Janene had been adamant, and it had taken her a lot of sign-language and patience to convey the message that she had no intention of arriving back in London looking like something from the *Arabian Nights*.

Last night's memories were still vivid in her mind, and she shuddered as she stirred her coffee. The escape from Hassan's 'love-nest' was something she'd never forget, and she still couldn't understand how Kassim had been able to find the place in that labyrinth of dark passageways and cleverly concealed doors.

It had been well after midnight when they'd arrived safely back at the house, but all her questions would be answered in the morning, he'd assured her. His immediate concern was for her to rest, and he'd brought a hot, sweet drink up to the room.

'This is a sedative,' he'd told her. 'It's herbal. There

will be no demons to plague you tonight. Forget Hassan. Sleep in peace.'

As she'd sat up in bed sipping the drink, a last shiver ran through her at the memory of that ugly, evil face. 'He—he was going to. . .'

Kassim had touched her shoulder gently. 'We can guess what his plans were for you. At this moment he is undoubtedly confessing his sins at the point of a knife. Now forget him.'

That was easier said than done. 'What—what will you do with him?' she had asked quietly.

'The Blue Men will take him back to their camp,' he'd growled. 'He will spend the remainder of his life as a slave to the women. He will do all the degrading menial work. The children will mock and revile him and at night he will sleep with the goats.' He'd paused and looked at her hopefully. 'Perhaps you think I am being too lenient with him?'

'No,' she'd said hastily. 'Sleeping with the goats sounds like just what he deserves.'

She'd finished her drink, then lain back. He'd kissed her tenderly on the forehead, then sat on the edge of the bed as if to guard and protect her for the rest of the night. Gratefully she'd closed her eyes. There were so many other questions she'd wanted to ask, but she'd been too tired.

She'd finished her breakfast and had just ordered a pot of fresh coffee when Kassim came striding in from the outer courtyard. As he took the seat opposite her his blue eyes studied her carefully. 'Good morning, little rose. Did you sleep well?'

'Yes. Very well, thanks.' Was it just her imagination or was that a look of strained tension on his face?

Perhaps he'd stayed awake all night. He certainly looked as if he had.

'I've been checking on the plane,' he announced casually. 'It's ready when you are. You should be back in London in time for a late lunch.' He paused and reached across the table for her hand. 'I'd still like to go with you, Janene. My offer to invest still stands. No strings attached. You said that you'd think about it.'

Her heart gave a lurch. After the events of last night, she knew with a blinding certainty that he was in love with her. And she also knew the reason why he could never marry her.

Well, what was so special about being married? The ghosts of her parents were no longer around to haunt her. Anyway, love was the thing that really mattered. It was obvious that they both wanted and needed one another. Was she going to be foolish enough to demand all or nothing?

'Yes, Kassim,' she murmured. 'I want you to come.'

He gave her hand a squeeze. 'Good. I don't deserve it, but you've made my sorrow easier to bear.'

She changed the subject quickly. 'Are you going to tell me how you managed to come to my rescue last night? Hassan seemed convinced that no one knew about the place.'

He gave a humourless smile. 'The ways of Allah are strange, indeed. He provided us with a guide. A blind beggar. He knew Hassan well and offered to help us.'

She blinked at him. 'Blind?'

He nodded. 'When Kebira rushed back to the house to tell us that you'd suddenly vanished from the face of the earth, I suspected Hassan at once.' He clenched his fists and his eyes became bleak. 'I was a fool. I knew he'd seek some way of getting his revenge but it never occurred to me that he'd seek it through you.'

An expression of torment lingered on his face for a moment, then he went on, 'I sent a messenger to fetch a dozen of my tribesmen. If necessary, we were going to take the town apart brick by brick until we found you. Kebira led us back to the spot where she'd last seen you. I and every servant from the house began searching and questioning as best we could. By the time the Blue Men arrived from the desert, everyone in town knew that I was hunting for Hassan. That was when the blind beggar came forward with his offer of help.' He smiled grimly at the recollection. 'Needless to say, he will never have to beg again. I have rewarded him with a pension which will keep him in comfort for the rest of his days.'

She still couldn't grasp it. 'But if he was blind. . .?'

Kassim gave a dry chuckle. 'When a man is deprived of his sight from birth, he develops his other senses. It may be his hearing. In the beggar's case it was his sense of smell. The old man told us that he always knew when Hassan was passing by the strong smell of cigar-smoke.'

'I can vouch for the stink,' Janene said grimly. 'He blew the damned fumes into my face. I was almost sick.'

'We should praise Allah that Hassan indulged in such a filthy habit,' Kassim said with a scowl. 'We took the beggar into the most likely-looking passageway. Although we could detect no smell of tobacco in the air, he managed to pick up the trail within half an hour. It seems that, over the months Hassan had been using the route to his secret hideaway, the very timbers and plaster of the walls had absorbed the tell-tale scent. The beggar literally sniffed his way to our quarry.'

'And what about the old woman?' Janene asked worriedly. 'I don't think she was really aware of what was going on. She doesn't deserve to be punished.'

Kassim put her mind at rest. 'She is being cared for by Sister Mary. A place will be found for her.'

She looked across the table into those amazing blue eyes and knew why she was so hopelessly, helplessly in love with him. It wasn't just his hatred of injustice and the ruthless way he dealt with evildoers. It was more to do with his sense of loyalty and the compassion he could show towards a blind beggar and an old woman. With all his power and wealth he could still take the time to care for the weak and defenceless.

A wry little smile touched her lips. 'Are you going to London dressed like that?'

He raised a dark, enquiring eyebrow. 'You would object to me entering one of your shops dressed in a blue cloak and black turban? Bad for business, perhaps?'

The truth was he looked so devilishly attractive that she felt like eating him. 'I've no objections whatsoever,' she murmured. 'But you might be a danger in traffic.'

He frowned. 'Why should I be a danger. . .?' He paused, then grinned. 'Forgive me. I am being more obtuse than usual this morning. However, to please you I shall change into something more appropriate when we are on the plane. My wardrobe is already aboard.'

Following Kassim's orders, the pilot had radioed ahead, and when they landed at Heathrow there was an embassy limousine and driver waiting for them. The

CD plates on the car guaranteed no trouble over passports, and would certainly solve the problem of parking in the West End, Janene told herself.

Before they got into the car she had to make a few phone calls until she was able to run Sally to ground, then she told the driver to head for the Kings Road in Chelsea.

Kassim had changed from his robes into an exquisitely tailored light grey suit, and as he sat next to her, long legs extended in the roomy interior and looking perfectly relaxed, she wondered yet again if she was doing the right thing by allowing this affair to continue.

Perhaps it was true that love was all that mattered, but the course they were now embarking on could only end in one way. The day would come when Kassim would want a son. That was the one thing all Moroccan men wanted. Sooner or later he'd have to choose a wife who was acceptable to his tribe, not an infidel like her. How long would it be until that day came? A year? Two years? And how would her heart stand it when he was forced to tell her that it was all over?

It still wasn't too late to change her mind. She could tell him right now that from here on their relationship was to be strictly business. After all, he'd been the one who'd made the 'no strings attached' offer, so he had no cause for complaint if she insisted on it. That was what a sensible woman would have done, but, as she'd acknowledged to herself more than once already, her brain went on holiday whenever he touched her.

She knew how he'd react if she told him of these feelings that were tormenting her. He'd simply take her in his arms, knock her senseless with a kiss and murmur softly in her ear about accepting the brief hours of happiness which Allah, in His wisdom, was granting them. And who was she to say that he was wrong?

As the limousine joined the heavy stream of traffic heading east into the city she had a sudden thought and she frowned at him. 'What happened to my own car? It was left at the cottage. It might have been stolen by now.'

He patted her thigh reassuringly. 'It is being cared for in a garage in Ashford. We can go there tomorrow and collect it.' He paused, and gave her the friendly-shark smile that always made her nerves ripple. 'Before we talk about anything else, I think we should discuss living arrangements while I'm in London. I don't intend to be parted from you for more than five minutes at a time while I'm here.'

Well, he couldn't have put it any clearer than that, she thought weakly. This was make her mind up time. Yes or no.

He watched the play of emotions on her face, then shrugged. 'Of course, if you insist on sleeping on your own I will respect your wishes. I'll book into my usual hotel, where I shall promptly tyrannise the staff and make everyone's life a misery, including my own.'

'Well, we can't have that, can we?' she replied lightly, avoiding the trap of looking into those eyes. 'I suppose you'll just have to share my flat.'

He patted her thigh again. 'Thank you. Your generosity is only exceeded by your beauty.'

'It's not very big, I'm afraid,' she murmured, still too embarrassed to make eye contact. 'And I've no servants at my beck and call. You'd have to help with the washing-up.'

'I'll buy you a dishwasher,' he said airily.

'I don't want a dishwasher. When you live on your own you don't need a dishwasher.'

He chuckled. 'Very well. You can wash and I'll dry.'

'Then there's the cleaning and dusting and polishing,' she pointed out. 'And there's the washing and ironing.'

He sighed. 'I see. Anything else? Leaking taps? Choked sinks?'

'Well. . .' she said thoughtfully, 'there are usually little odd jobs that need doing around the place. A squeaky door-hinge to be oiled. A plug needing a new fuse. A shelf to be put up. A bathroom tile to be replaced.'

He nodded. 'And when all these little odd jobs have been attended to?'

'Then we can sit and relax with a drink,' she said cheerfully.

'I'm more likely to fall asleep with exhaustion,' he observed drily.

'Oh, I doubt that,' she murmured. 'I won't let you work that hard.'

He growled at her good-naturedly, 'No woman in history has ever tried to domesticate a Berber. If word of this ever gets back to Morocco, my reputation will be in ruins.'

She smiled back at him, afraid of his eyes no longer. 'Don't worry, Kassim. It'll be our little secret.'

'It had better be,' he threatened blithely. He glanced at his watch, then picked up the intercom and ordered the driver to leave the motorway at the next junction. At her look of enquiry he explained, 'In return for your generous offer of hospitality I'm going to buy you a present. Now, please don't argue. I am feeling particularly kind-hearted today and you'd be foolish not to take advantage of it.'

She smiled at him, then said drily, 'If this is a trick to get out of the housework, you're wasting your money.'

They were passing a rather up-market and expensive dress boutique when he ordered the driver to stop. Taking her by the arm, he marched her inside.

At the sight of him the two young girl assistants looked at him breathlessly, then the faster of the two tripped forward and said huskily, 'May I help you, sir?'

Kassim gave her a thousand-watt smile. 'I certainly hope so. This lady requires something suitable to wear for a lunch-date. Something the same shade as her eyes, I think. Can you manage that?'

'Yes, sir.' The girl reluctantly tore her gaze away from him and studied Janene briefly. 'If you would kindly step this way, madam.'

Janene tried on four dresses but none of them pleased him. As she stepped out of the changing-booth for the fifth time, in a two-piece suit in emerald-green with white piping, he nodded in satisfaction. 'Leave it on,' he commanded, then, while he wrote out a cheque, her discarded skirt and blouse were parcelled up by the other assistant.

When they were back in the car he studied her again in approval. 'That suit must have been made with you in mind. The colour is exactly right and it tempts the eye to the hidden treasure beneath.'

'So you're a fashion expert now?' she murmured, hiding her pleasure behind a façade of light mockery.

'No,' he answered back. 'Simply a man who knows what he likes. All you need now is an emerald necklace to hang round that pretty neck. We'll stop at the first——'

'Oh, no, we won't,' she said firmly. 'One present is enough. Anyway, we don't have the time. Sally is waiting. We have to pick her up, then we can all lunch together and discuss taking you on as a silent partner.'

He looked at her shrewdly. 'Do I detect an anxious note in your voice. . .the merest hint of apprehension in those delightful eyes?'

'Yes.' She sighed. 'You probably do. I didn't mention anything about you to Sally over the phone. I just said that I wanted to meet her for lunch. When I turn up with you she's bound to ask a lot of awkward questions about who you are. How did we meet? How long have I known you?'

'Just tell her the truth,' he suggested nonchalantly.

She almost laughed aloud. 'The truth? She'd never believe it. And I wouldn't blame her.' She thought for a moment, then shrugged. 'I suppose I'll have to. But I'm not sure how she'll take to the idea of having a ruthless operator like you for a partner.'

He examined his fingernails and drawled, 'I shall simply stand with my head bowed and try my best to look humble.'

She eyed him doubtfully. Kassim Riffik trying to look humble? This she had to see.

When they reached the shop in the busy Kings Road, the driver ignored the 'no parking' signs and brought the limousine to a halt outside the front door. As Kassim made to rise Janene touched his arm and smiled quickly. 'There's no need for us both to go in. You stay here while I fetch Sally.'

His blue eyes shimmered with amusement. 'As you

wish. I dare say you want to warn her about me. Prepare her for the worst?'

'Yes,' she muttered. 'Something like that. After all, you are the kind of man women warn their daughters about.'

Before he could come back at her with some flippant retort, she opened her door and dashed across the pavement.

Sally, needless to say, welcomed her with a warm hug, then frowned over her shoulder. 'I wouldn't park there, Janene. The wheel-clampers are like locusts around here.'

'They can't touch that car,' she said lightly. 'It has CD plates from the Moroccan embassy.'

Sally's eyes widened in surprise, then widened even further as she went to the door. 'Oh! Be still, my aching heart! Who but who is that gorgeous-looking devil in the back seat? Is he real or just a figment of my imagination? He can't be your fiancé. You told me that Damien had brown hair.'

'I'm finished with Damien,' Janene said calmly. 'That's why I came in on my own. To warn you. That man out there gets twitchy at the sound of Damien's name. Now, it's a very long, involved story and we haven't got time to go into it right now. That man in the car is Kassim Riffik. He's having lunch with us, and if we don't get a move on it'll be too late. Lunchtime will be over.'

'Is he an Arab?' Sally asked, too engrossed in the handsome profile to listen.

'That's another thing,' she cautioned. 'Don't call him an Arab. He's a Berber. It seems to make a big difference to him.'

'Hmm. . .' Sally turned with a conspiratorial smile. 'Are you and he. . .? You know. . .have you got a thing going?'

Janene sighed. 'Yes. I suppose we have. I'll tell you about it later.' Well, some of it at least, she amended to herself.

Sally's eyes lit up with anticipation. 'You'd better. I want to hear every savoury little detail.' She called her assistant through from the stock-room to take charge of the counter, then she grabbed her shoulder-bag and followed Janene outside.

Gallantly, Kassim had emerged from the car to greet them, and she watched the expression on Sally's face with amusement as he turned his charm to full blast. Taking Sally's hand, he raised it to his lips and smiled at them both. 'In the company of two such beautiful young ladies, I will be the envy of every man in London.'

They went to a little restaurant Janene knew in Knightsbridge, and when they'd given their orders to the waiter she got straight to the point. 'Sally, do you still want me back in partnership with you?'

'Of course I do,' Sally replied in obvious delight. 'I need you. Things aren't the same without you around.'

She smiled. 'That's settled, then.' She heard Kassim clear his throat and she took a deep breath. 'And how would you feel about taking on a third partner?'

The sharp business side of Sally took over, and her expression became guarded. 'Who do you have in mind?'

'Me,' said Kassim, his smile open and friendly.

Sally looked at him in surprise. 'Oh. . .'

'He only wants to invest some money in the business.

Help us expand,' Janene said quickly. 'We'd still be running it.' She could see the look of doubt on Sally's face and she smoothed things over. 'Don't think about it now. Let's have our lunch in peace. We'll discuss it when we go back to the shop. I have some samples I want you to look at.'

Kassim broke in, 'Sally's hesitation is only natural. Although she is burning with curiosity, she knows nothing about me. One does not take on a partner without knowing his character and background. I certainly wouldn't. Perhaps you could begin by telling her where and how we met.'

He was pushing it, Janene thought angrily. Why couldn't he just keep quiet and leave her to deal with this problem in her own way? But that was asking too much, wasn't it? He wasn't the type of man to beat around the bush. His idea of breaking the ice was to hit you with a flame-thrower.

'Should I give her the unexpurgated edition or the cleaned-up version?' she asked coldly.

His thin lips stretched in a confident smile and his blue eyes taunted her mercilessly. 'Just tell the truth, Janene. There should be no secrets between partners.'

She smiled back at him sweetly. 'Very well. Should I begin with the night we met at the party, or should I skip that bit and go on to the night you drugged and kidnapped me and spirited me off to your kasbah in Morocco?'

That didn't go down well with Sally, who eyed her sternly across the table and reprimanded, 'I thought we were having a serious discussion here?'

'We are,' Janene assured her gravely. 'I'd hoped that

we could put this off till later, but it seems that I'm being outvoted.'

Kassim broke in with a pleasant smile and an easy drawl. 'When my reputation and honesty are called into question I don't believe in wasting time. To put the record straight—as far as the kidnapping charge is concerned, it's a mere technicality. The truth is that Janene already belonged to me. I'd paid a lot of money for her and I saved her from making a fool of herself over her ex-fiancé.

She saw the dazed, uncomprehending look on Sally's face, and she said weakly, 'I—I warned you that it was a very long, involved story, didn't I?'

'Yes,' Sally said drily. 'So you did.' She smiled politely. 'This may sound like a stupid question, but. . . when is all this supposed to have taken place?'

'Just over a week ago,' Janene admitted, realising how preposterous the whole thing sounded.

Sally nodded to herself. 'I see. Well, a week isn't very long, is it? I mean. . .how well can you get to know someone in a week?' She smiled an apology at Kassim. 'No offence meant.'

'None taken,' he assured her lightly. 'You are a cautious and shrewd businesswoman. If I do invest in your business, at least I know it will be in safe hands.'

Sally acknowledged the compliment with a gracious nod and Janene said impatiently, 'Please, just take my word for it, Sally. I'd never have brought Kassim here if I didn't trust him. And he's right. He really did save me from making a fool of myself.'

'This gets more intriguing by the minute,' Sally murmured. 'I can't wait to hear the rest. But perhaps you're right. We'll discuss it all after lunch. In private.'

Kassim looked at Janene pointedly and said, 'Such a discussion may not be necessary. If Sally doesn't like the samples you've brought, then there is no need for me to prolong my visit here.'

Consternation flickered briefly in her eyes but she managed to keep her voice even. 'You mean you'd no longer be interested in a partnership?'

'I'm afraid not,' he drawled. 'I'm prepared to invest money if it helps to provide work for the people of my town, but not otherwise.'

For a moment she felt numb with shock and disappointment, then it passed and she dredged up a smile. 'I understand. I suppose that's a perfectly reasonable attitude.'

When the meal arrived she found that she'd lost her appetite, and she hid her bitterness behind a torrent of inconsequential chit-chat.

An hour later they were back at the shop in the Kings Road. Sally closed the door of her office firmly behind her, then smiled briskly at both of them. 'Right, let's get this over and done with, then we can all relax.'

Janene opened the case and began setting out the contents on the desk-top. Everything had been tagged with the wholesale price, and Sally examined each item closely. Finally she looked up at Janene and nodded. 'I'm impressed. I've never seen anything like that silver jewellery. And the colours and needlework on those blouses and scarves is brilliant.'

Janene heaved a sigh of relief. Mostly it was because of the satisfaction of knowing that her own judgement had been proved right. But a little part of it could have been something else. Something shameful. Like knowing that she and Kassim could still. . . She pushed that

thought out of her mind and smiled at Sally. 'Good!'
she said brightly. 'With the money that Kassim is willing
to invest, we can expand out of London. We could
open a couple of branches in the Midlands. . .'

Sally shook her head. 'Not so fast, Janene. I haven't
quite made up my mind yet about Mr Riffik.' She
smiled politely at Kassim and he smiled back politely in
return.

'You said that the story was long and invovled,' Sally
reminded her. 'Could you shorten it?' Just tell me the
really juicy parts. But be tasteful. I'm still relatively
young and innocent.'

Janene eyed her again with impatience. She knew
that Sally was merely toying with her, but two could
play at that game. With a dramatic sigh of resignation
she said, 'Very well. . .if you insist.' She drew a deep
breath and launched herself into a frenetic
recitation. . .

'I first met Kassim at a party. He'd come to London
because his nephew had been cheated at a crooked
gambling-club in Soho. Damien had been responsible
for that, and Kassim wanted the money back, but when
he saw me he decided that I would do instead. Of
course, I never knew anything about this at the time.

'Anyway, at the party Kassim came on pretty strong
about raging volcanoes of fire and passion, and about
how he wanted to steal me away in the night and make
wild, passionate love to me in his tent under the stars,
but I told him no thanks, because I was engaged to be
married.

'Then, a couple of nights later, I fell asleep by the
fire in my cottage in Kent and when I woke up I was in
his private plane and when we landed he took me to his

"tent" which is really the most fabulous house you've ever seen. I was scared at first, but he treated me like a princess and I even had a personal maid called Kebira. Then, after I went to the souk with Kebira and an ex-nun called Sister Mary, we got back to the house in time to find Kassim, who is kind of Lord Mayor over there, passing judgement on a pig of a man called Hassan, who'd divorced three wives for being barren when it was his fault all the time.

'Then Kassim took me to see the Blue Men. They are his tribe who live in the desert. On the way there we got caught in this terrible sandstorm and on the way back I got blisters on my feet and heatstroke, but Kassim got me home, put me to bed and gave me lots of loving tender care.'

She paused for a moment and noted with satisfaction the way Sally's mouth was hanging open, then she went on blithely, 'A couple of days after that I was at the market with Kebira when someone dragged me into an alley, threw a dirty sack over my head and led me to this secret apartment. There was a huge bedroom. . . all silk and perfume and disgusting statues and pictures, and I was nearly sick. Then that horrible Hassan came in and told me that I was to be a sex-slave to entertain his friends for the next two years. It was his way of getting his revenge on Kassim. I was there for hours and was beginning to get really desperate when Kassim and some of his tribe came to my rescue. They had been led to the place by an old blind beggar. The Blue Men took Hassan away to be their women's slave and sleep with the goats, and Kassim took me home. That was last night. This morning he brought me back to London in his private jet and here I am.'

She turned to Kassim. 'I haven't forgotten anything, have I?'

Suppressing the laughter that was threatening to erupt from his mouth, he growled, 'Only the passionate nights. . .and the day at the beach, when we tried that special treatment and you——'

'Yes. Quite,' she said hurriedly.

'In that case, I think you've covered all the relevant facts.'

Behind the desk Sally's face was a picture of awe and disbelief. At last she smiled weakly. 'Are you going to have all that set to music? It would be a sure-fire hit in the West End.'

'I told you that she wouldn't believe me,' Janene complained to Kassim. 'And instead of looking humble, as you promised, you're standing there with a big grin on your face!'

Sally got to her feet. 'All right! I believe you. My God, it's too far-fetched to be anything but the truth!'

Janene smiled with relief. 'Well, now that your curiosity has been satisfied and I've proved that Kassim isn't an out-and-out rogue, can we come to some decision about taking him on as a partner?'

Sally took an infuriatingly long time about it. First she removed her glasses. Then she polished them carefully with a handkerchief. Then she put them back on and studied Kassim in silence.

Kassim gazed back at her calmly and Janene wondered at his stoic patience over all this vacillation. With all his wealth he could buy and sell the pair of them a hundred times over. Sally was walking on eggs and she didn't know it. He'd never been treated like this in his life. No one would have dared. Least of all a woman.

Any second now, he was liable to let rip with some ferocious expletive and storm out of the shop.

At last Sally nodded and smiled at her. 'I'd be honoured to have him as a partner, Janene. On one condition.'

She eyed Sally warily. 'We're lucky to get him, Sally. I don't think a "condition" is a very good idea.'

'This one is,' Sally said cheerfully. Smiling at Kassim, she said, 'If you're so smart, you must be able to see that Janene is madly in love with you. That being the case, I insist that you propose to her here and now.'

The sheer audacity of it took Janene's breath away and she looked quickly at Kassim, then felt her heart plummet as she saw the hard, bleak expression settle over his face.

'You ask the impossible,' he said grimly. 'I can never offer my hand in marriage to Janene. She must look elsewhere for a husband.'

Although she'd known it all along, that didn't prevent the knife from being driven a little deeper into Janene's heart as she heard the cold, fateful words come from his own lips.

With a smile of calm resignation she explained the situation to Sally. 'Kassim can't marry me. He needs a wife who is acceptable to his tribe. Apparently, I'm not.'

Sally reared up, affronted. 'You're not!' She turned on Kassim and demanded, 'What's wrong with her?'

A slight furrow had appeared on his brow, and in a vocie of steely civility he said, 'This is something that has to be discussed between Janene and me. I would be forever in your debt if you would grant us a few minutes in private.'

'Yes, of course,' Sally said agreeably. 'Take the rest

of the afternoon if you need it. Just so long as we get a happy ending to all this.'

As soon as they were alone, his frown deepened and he questioned her harshly, 'Who said that you weren't acceptable to my tribe?'

She blinked at him, taken aback by his tone, and muttered, 'No one needed to. It became quite obvious after what Hassan said to me.'

'Hassan!' His face darkened in fury. 'What does that piece of gutter-trash have to do with this? I'll have his genitals eaten by ants when I return.'

She waited until the storm of his anger had died down, then she said calmly, 'He was the one who told me about the tradition in your tribe. If the chief wishes to marry, he must present the woman to the tribe and get their approval. Especially if the woman is an infidel like me.'

Kassim nodded. 'For once in his life, at least, that foul wretch spoke the truth.'

She shrugged despondently. 'Well, that's that, then. They certainly gave me the once-over when I arrived at their oasis. Every one of them got in line to look me up and down, didn't they?'

'And they liked what they saw,' he growled. 'Just as I knew they would.'

'Yes,' she countered. 'But obviously not enough to allow you to marry me.' She bit her lip and averted her eyes. 'I know that it isn't your fault, Kassim. You've got a position to maintain. You can't go against the wishes of your people.'

'The wishes of my people were that you and I should have a long and happy life,' he assured her vigorously. 'A life blessed with many children.'

'Oh. . .' Her eyes widened and she could feel a tiny, rapid pulse in her throat as she looked up at him. 'Wh—why didn't you tell me? Or. . .did you just change your mind?'

His hands gripped her shoulders fiercely, his fingers digging deep. 'I didn't tell you then, Janene, because I was a romantic fool. The front seat of a Land Rover jolting across the desert is not the appropriate place to ask for a woman's hand in marriage. I wanted to wait until that evening. There, by the pool, with the moonlight in your hair and the starlight in your eyes, I would have declared my undying love and asked you to be my wife.'

She swallowed the enormous lump in her throat and stumbled over the words. 'I—I had no idea that you. . . felt like that about me.'

'Of course you didn't,' he said softly. 'And I didn't know what your feelings were towards me at the time. We had made love, it is true. But was that enough?' He paused, and she saw the tormented anger in his eyes as he went on, 'And then it all went wrong. In my foolishness I said something to upset you, and you leapt out of the Land Rover before I could stop you.'

'I was the one who was foolish,' she pointed out. 'I should have listened to your warning.'

He shook his head adamantly. 'You are a strong-willed woman, Janene. Nevertheless, you were my responsibility and I neglected my duty. In my arrogance I sought to teach you a lesson in respect. Not respect for me, but for the dangers of the desert. But I carried the lesson too far and you suffered as a consequence. I can never forgive myself for that.'

'But you weren't to blame!' she insisted. 'I just got what I deserved for not —'

He went on as if he hadn't heard her. 'The very next day you told me that you wanted to return to London.'

Her mind raced desperately. She hadn't known that he loved her when she'd said that. She'd tried to find out the previous night, but her oblique questioning had drawn a blank. According to him, she was merely the spoils of war, a woman to be rescued — worth her weight in diamonds, perhaps, but there had not been one single mention of love.

'Under the circumstances I couldn't refuse your request,' he went on. 'I knew I had no right to ask you to spend the rest of your life with a man who was incapable of looking after you.'

His words of bitter self-recrimination stirred a memory of something he'd said before: 'A man who fails to provide for the comfort and security of his woman is not worthy of the name.' That had been the day they'd been at the beach. She'd made some joking remark about his not having checked personally to ensure that there was food in the Land Rover before they'd left the house. He'd really taken it to heart and she hadn't understood his unexpected reaction.

He was still taking it hard, by the look on his face, and as she eyed him in exasperation he continued, 'As if I hadn't harmed you enough, I compounded my failings by allowing you to fall into the clutches of that evil worm Hassan. For that alone I should be scourged by all the demons in the seven pits of Shaitan.'

In spite of his tirade of self-abasement he bore himself wiht all the dignity and courage of a man in front of a firing-squad, disdainfully scorning a blindfold.

She continued to look at him in despair. Honour and pride were admirable qualities in a man, but when they stood in the way of true love something had to go. And that was just as true for her as it was for him.

Swallowing her own pride, she bared her innermost soul in a voice that trembled with emotion. 'You're hurting me now much more than the desert or Hassan ever did, Kassim. You were quick enough to put salve on my feet, but the pain in my heart means nothing to you.'

His grip became even tighter and he looked genuinely puzzled. 'Why should your heart be pained? I don't understand. It's beyond belief that any woman could love a man who keeps putting her life in danger.'

'I suppose it seems that way to you,' she murmured. 'Just as I ask myself how a man could ever love a woman who's too feather-brained to look after herself. But love hasn't got anything to do with being sensible, has it?'

His hands dropped to her waist and he pulled her closer against himself. His sapphire eyes swept over her face and his features softened. 'You're as foolish as I am, little rose.'

'I know I am. . .darling,' she whispered up at him huskily. 'And I think that we fools should stick together, don't you?'

A sigh of relief and pleasure escaped his lips. 'You have put the light back into my life, Englishwoman. Allah must have guided me to you.'

Her eyes twinkled up at him in happiness. 'Then ask Him to guide your lips to mine, right now. I want one of your long, passionate kisses. And, when it's over, we'll go through and tell Sally the good news.'

# CHAPTER ELEVEN

FOR a few minutes the western sky was gloriously ablaze with orange and crimson fire, then the sun dipped below the horizon and night came swiftly to the desert. One by one the stars winked into life and the moon hung suspended overhead like a huge silver sickle.

In a vast circle around the oasis, camp-fires were lit by the Blue Men, who would keep a ceremonial guard on this, their chief's wedding-night. At the moment Kassim was visiting each of his tribesmen in turn, praising them and thanking them for their loyalty. It was a gesture typical of Kassim, and one which would be appreciated and remembered in years to come.

In the huge, luxuriously furnished tent which had been set up beneath the palm-trees, Kebira gave a few more gentle brush-strokes to her mistress's red hair and said haltingly, 'Have. . .having patience. Kassim. . . your husband. . .here soon.'

Janene bestowed a smile of encouragement on her maid. 'Very good, Kebira. You are a quick learner. You'll be speaking English fluently in a few months.'

It had been Kassim's wish that the wedding should take place at the oasis, among his people, and he'd started making the arrangements the moment they'd arrived back from London.

Sally had flown back with them to be the maid of honour and, during the three days it had taken Kassim to contact his army of relatives from all over North

Africa, France and Spain, Janene had taken the opportunity to show her partner around the town.

The noise, colours and sights of the souk had fascinated Sally, but she'd been even more intrigued by the four tall, mysterious figures in blue cloaks and black turbans who were never more than half a dozen steps behind.

Over the next couple of days, as guests kept arriving and the house began filling up, Janene had spent most of her time being introduced to and entertaining a never-ending stream of Kassim's uncles, aunts, cousins and brothers. She'd been a little apprehensive at first, but she was soon put at her ease by their friendly smiles and enthusiastic embraces. It certainly didn't seem to bother them that the head of their family had decided to marry an Anglo-Saxon infidel. On the contrary. They seemed to be a lot more cosmopolitan in their attitudes than many of the people she knew back home.

When she'd awakened that morning, it was to find Kassim had already left for the oasis to check on the final arrangements. There were no dusty, bumpy rides in the Land Rover to be endured this time. By helicopter, the trip to the oasis would take less than half an hour, and two had been hired to ferry everyone there and back in relays.

Janene had been on the last trip to leave the house, along with Sally, Kebira and Sister Mary, who'd turned up at the last minute. Breathless with excitement, the older woman had boarded the helicopter, strapped herself into the next seat, and explained about the slight problem at the medical centre, then added brightly, 'Sure, and I wouldn't want to be missing this grand occasion. Haven't I just been looking forward to the day when he takes himself a wife and settles down.'

The remark had jogged something in Janene's memory and she'd smiled at Mary and said casually, 'You've lived here a long time, haven't you, Mary? I suppose by now that you're familiar with all the local customs?'

Mary had nodded. 'That I am. And pretty strange some of them are, too, I can tell you. But I never interfere. After all, it's their country, not mine.'

'Quite. So when I first told you that Kassim was taking me to see the Blue Men, you must have known that he had marriage in mind.'

Mary had smiled and bobbed her head. 'I had a good idea.'

'Yes. But you never let on to me, did you?' Janene had pointed out in mild accusation. 'You said that it was probably just to see how they lived out in the desert.'

'Well, now. . .' Mary had said, quite unabashed. 'The first time we met, you were wearing an engagement-ring. And the second time, when you asked me about the Blue Men, you weren't. Sure, and I didn't know what to think, so I just decided to keep my mouth shut about the custom. But I was sure that things would sort themselves out in the end, and they have, haven't they?'

She'd smiled with affection at the older woman. 'Yes, Mary. I think they have.'

The ceremony had taken place an hour after they'd landed at the oasis. In the tent set aside for the purpose Janene had changed into her bridal outfit: a robe and head-dress of shimmering white silk with gold edging.

Kebira had fussed around her in a fever of excitement, making sure that every detail was perfect, then Sally and a retinue of women from the tribe had led her to Kassim's side. Shaded from the sun by a large canopy which had been erected between the trees, she'd listened to the strange Berber words of the ceremony which would bind them together as man and wife.

The rest of day had been given over to feasting and general enjoyment, but now all the guests had departed back to town, and night and serenity had come to the desert.

Kebira had been humming softly to herself, but suddenly she laid the hairbrush down and gazed out into the moonlit oasis. 'I think. . .I hear something. . .'

Janene looked at her maid hopefully. 'Is it Kassim?'

Kebira waited for a tense moment, straining her eyes towards the dark shadows beneath the trees, then she smiled and said excitedly, 'Your husband. . .he is near.'

Dry-mouthed and with a quickening heart, Janene rose from the pile of cushions she'd been perched on for the last half-hour.

Suddenly the tall, blue-cloaked figure of Kassim was framed in the entrance. In the light of the oil-lamps his strong features were the colour of dark copper, and his lips stretched in a white, dazzling smile. As he stepped forward Kebira gave a quick bow, then quietly left the tent.

For a few moments he seemed content to stand in silence, his eyes almost luminous as they drank in the sight of her, then at last he spoke softly. 'Well, my little rose, we are alone at last. Come to me. I want to smell the perfume of your hair and taste the sweet honey of your lips. Duty has deprived me of these pleasures for too long.'

Gliding forward, she melted into his strong embrace and shivered with delicious abandon at the sweet tenderness of his kiss. His hands moulded her perfectly to the length of his body in anticipation of delights to come, and the power drained from her limbs, leaving her limp with aching desire.

His lips reluctantly left hers and he whispered huskily, 'If Allah would but grant me one wish, I would command the very stars to halt in their courses so that this one night would last until the end of time.' He gazed down into the emerald depths of her eyes and sighed. 'But since He has more to worry about than a fool such as I, we shall have to be content with what He has already granted us.'

He gave her another lingering kiss, then he released her. Striding over to the rear wall of the tent, he threw aside a silk drape to reveal a cool-box. Inside, packed in ice, were two bottles and glasses. Holding the bottles aloft and grinning at her astonished expression, he said, 'All it takes is foresight and ingenuity. After all, what is a wedding-night without champagne? There are some western customs of which I thoroughly approve, and this is one of them.' He poured two brimming glasses, then handed her one. 'I'm sorry there isn't any caviare.'

'Good,' she said, making a face. 'I hate the stuff.' She sipped the drink, then smiled. 'But this, I like.'

'I knew you would,' he said modestly. 'Champagne was made for beautiful women like you and nights like this.'

Sipping at his own drink, he led her outside and they stood in silent admiration of the splendour of the night sky. The air was still and pleasantly cool after the heat of the day. A distant sound of laughter came from the cluster of tents at the far side of the oasis. Celebrations would go on over there until the small hours.

She sipped at her drink again, then said quietly, 'It's strange. I remember the first night we met. You told me that you'd like to take me to your tent in the desert. I thought you were joking.'

A troubled frown settled on his face and he looked down at her. 'You would have preferred a hotel suite in Paris? Or Rome?'

She shook her head, reached up and pressed her finger to his lips. 'Darling, right now I wouldn't trade this tent for the top floor of the Dorchester in London.'

His lips nibbled hungrily at her fingertip, then he gave a grunt of approval. 'Those are the words I hoped to hear. You spoke like a true Berber woman.'

He started nibbling her finger again and she revelled in the feeling of titillation, then murmured, 'Yes. Well, I suppose I am a Berber woman now.' She revelled in the feeling a moment longer, then withdrew her hand.

'The green fields and leafy lanes of England are only a few hours' flight from here,' he reminded her gently. 'We will be making frequent trips there. I realise that there may be things you miss from time to time. You may go on your own if you should so desire. Always remember, little rose, that wedding-ring is a symbol of love and trust. It was never intended to shackle you to a prison wall.'

His words touched her heart more than she'd thought possible, and she swallowed to relieve the tightness in her throat. 'I never want to be on my own again, darling. A woman needs a husband and her place is by his side. There was a time when I'd have argued against that, but I hadn't met you then.' She sipped her drink again, then changed the subject to something that had been preying on her mind. 'Did I meet all your relatives today, darling? I'm talking about your nephew—the one who lost all his money gambling.'

The blue eyes looked at her sharply. 'No. He is no longer welcome in this family. His mother was here, but he is where he belongs—cleaning the kitchen floors of a hotel in Tangier.'

She looked up at him, her eyes unwavering. 'I know that it isn't any of my business, darling, but couldn't you find it in your heart to forgive him? Take him back into the family again?'

'Do you wish me to?' His tone suggested that his only desire in life was to please her.

She nodded vigorously. 'Yes. I believe you should.'

'Then it shall be done,' he pronounced. For a moment he gazed up at the stars, as if the answer to the eccentricity of the female mind could be found up there, then he smiled down at her, his mildly puzzled eyes sweeping her face. 'Your concern for a complete stranger does you credit, but would you mind telling me why you should feel any pity for a foolish youth like him?'

'Well,' she said simply, 'we've all done foolish things at some time in our lives, haven't we? And he wasn't really bad, was he? He was a victim. And I know that it probably sounds stupid, but because of my relationship with Damien I feel a little bit responsible.' She bit her lip and frowned at him. 'Does that make sense to you?'

'Yes, little rose,' he admitted. 'It makes sense. You

feel guilt by association, though you shouldn't.' He pursed his lips thoughtfully, then added, 'Anyway, it may be that he has already learnt by his mistake. In future he will be more cautious in his dealings with strangers.'

'There's also another reason,' she added quietly. 'We owe him a debt of gratitude. If it hadn't been for him, you would never have come to London and you and I would never have met.'

His teeth gleamed again in his dark features as he laughed. 'By the beard of the Prophet! You are absolutely right! Perhaps Allah merely used him as an unwitting pawn in His great design. He must indeed be rewarded. Instead of scrubbing floors, he will take over as manager of our new hotel in Agadir.' He took her by the hand. 'Come. Let us find out what further treasures my generous spirit has to offer.'

In the tent he refilled their glasses, then gestured to the pile of cushions. 'They are as impatient for the feel of your smooth skin as I am, but we shall enjoy the pleasures of wine and conversation first. We shall gaze into each other's eyes like two love-sick calves and we shall tease each other unmercifully until the blood is pounding in our veins and our very souls are on fire for——'

'You'd better not wait too long,' she warned with a smile. 'My teasing threshold is very low when I'm around you. I'm liable to forget that I'm a lady and take a flying leap at you.'

'That would be an interesting experience,' he mused aloud. 'I would have no choice but to surrender immediately, of course. Now, are there any more favours, demands, wishes or requests you want to make? Anything that is within my power to give is yours for the asking.'

'I want to learn to speak Berber.'

He inclined his head. 'That's good. But it will have to wait until tomorrow. Tonight we speak only the language of love.' He gave a humorous smile. 'Anything else?'

She sipped her drink and looked at him thoughtfully. 'Just one last thing, darling.'

'Name it, and it shall be yours.'

She laid down her glass and smiled at him lazily through half-closed eyes. 'Will you please get rid of that damn drink and take me in your arms? I'm already past that threshold I was talking about.'

'Yes,' he murmured softly, 'I think you're right. We are wasting too much time in foolishness.' Reaching for her, he drew her closer until their lips met. His robe unwound and drifted to the floor as he undid the golden clip at her shoulder, and as his hand slipped under her flimsy bra to cup and caress her breast she moved her mouth over his in frenzied abandon.

He eased her briefs over her slim hips and she kicked them off. As his hand continued to fondle her breast, her own hands began hurriedly undressing him. Clinging to each other, they sank slowly on to the cushions, and the long night of exquisite lovemaking began. . .

Kassim drove the hired Mercedes saloon while Janene sat in the rear seat with the baby cradled in her arms. The quiet country lanes of Kent rolled by, and she leaned forward. 'There's a junction coming up. Take a left turn when you get to it.'

Soon, the square Norman tower of the church

became visible above the hedgerows and she leaned forward again and tapped his shoulder. 'There it is.'

In her arms the baby stirred and opened his eyes and smiled as if he knew that they were almost at the end of their journey. They were wonderful blue eyes, just like Kassim's, she thought. And the same raven-black hair.

There was no one else in sight when Kassim drew the car up at the churchyard. Carefully carrying the huge bunch of fresh flowers they'd bought in Ashford, he opened the rear door and helped her out. Still holding the baby tightly, she straightened up and looked around. The sight of the well-tended graveyard filled her momentarily with sad, heart-wrenching memories, then she cast them aside and made her way slowly along the narrow, gravelled path. Kassim followed a few steps behind.

Among the ancient, weatherbeaten headstones, the newer one marking her parents' grave was easy to find. Stopping before it, she closed her eyes and prayed in silence for a few moments. Kassim placed the flowers at the foot of the headstone, then stepped back as she knelt down and laid the baby on the soft carpet of grass. He smiled up at her, gurgling with pleasure, his tiny limbs waving and kicking in the air.

As she stood up Kassim gave her a smile of encouragement, and she cleared her throat and began talking in a soft, quiet voice. 'Hello, Mum. Hello, Dad. I don't suppose you expected me. It's been a while, and you probably thought I'd forgotten all about you. Well, I haven't and I never will. I've come here to let you see your first grandson. His name is Kamal and he's just gorgeous, isn't he? And this big, handsome devil standing next to me is Kassim, his father. We were married just over a year ago. He's a wonderful man. You'd have liked him a lot. He's always kind and thoughtful. In fact, it was his idea to bring Kamal here.

'We live in Morocco most of the time, although I'm still in business with Sally. I'm the buyer for our chain of boutiques. I don't need the money, but it helps the people in our town.

'We've decided that when Kamal is old enough he'll be educated here, in England. Then he'll study medicine or law. Anyway, we'll let him choose that for himself. But I know that one day we're all going to be very, very proud of him.'

She reached for Kassim's hand and pressed it, then went on, 'Kassim is very good to me. No woman could ask for a better husband. He wants a big family, so I think you'll be seeing a lot of us over the next few years. Perhaps the next one will be a girl.'

She smiled up at Kassim. 'Is there anything you'd like to say, darling?'

'Not at the moment,' he said quietly. 'I think they're too busy talking to their grandson.'

She looked down at the grass. Their son had stopped his gurgling and kicking. Now his eyes were tightly closed and he seemed for all the world to be frowning in concentration.

The sight amused her and she laughed. 'I think you're right.'

He took her into his arms tenderly and grinned. 'Who knows what they may be talking about? I think we should leave them undisturbed for the next few minutes.'

'Anything you say, darling,' she whispered, smiling up at those blue eyes. 'We're not in any hurry, are we?'

'Tell me,' he asked quietly, 'is a man allowed to kiss the woman he loves in a place like this?'

'Oh, yes,' she said lightly. 'By all means. In fact, it's an old English tradition. Quiet spots like this are favourite meeting-places for courting couples.'

His blue eyes gleamed in pleasure. 'Well, if it's an old tradition we must do our best to keep it alive. We will court while our son listens to the wisdom of his grandparents.'

The slight whimper was enough to jerk Kassim instantly awake. Careful not to wake Janene, he slipped out of bed, crossed over silently to the crib and gently lifted his son into his arms. Kamal's blue eyes opened and gazed up at him. There was a tiny smile of recognition, then a burble of happiness, and the eyes closed once more.

Soundlessly he carried him across the room towards the open window, where the air was cooler, and began rocking him gently. It was all the travelling which had upset the baby's routine, he told himself. Tomorrow everything would be back to normal.

The stars were reflected in the still waters of the pool in the courtyard below. All was peace and tranquillity, and Kassim smiled as he recalled the very different scene here when Kamal had been born in this very room.

As Janene's time had drawn near, the Blue Men and their families had moved in from the desert and set up camp on the outskirts of the town, in preparation for the big event.

Kassim had delivered her baby with the help of Sister Mary, and it was a moment that would live in his heart forever: the joy of holding his new-born son and the feeling of overwhelming love and tenderness as Janene had reached and taken it to her breast.

As the news quickly spread, the town had immediately put up shutters and declared a three-day festival. That same night the Blue Men and their wives had come to the house. In reverential silence and bearing gifts, the men had filed in to pay homage to their future chief. After they had gone it was the women's turn, and they'd gone into raptures of delight over the infant.

Later, the feasting and the music and the dancing had taken place in the courtyard below. At the height of the celebrations Janene had joined him with their infant son in their arms, and together they'd stood at this very window, acknowledging the cheers and shouts of congratulation from the crowd.

By now the echoes of that night had faded into the past. Kassim stood for a few minutes more, then, sure that Kamal was soundly asleep once more, he carried him over to his crib.

Janene was lying on her back, one arm outstretched, her breasts rising and falling as she slept. The silk sheet had slipped, uncovering most of her naked length, but he was in no hurry to cover her up. This was a game he often played in the quiet hours of the night. Just gazing down at her like this, knowing that this wonderful woman belonged to him as much as he belonged to her. In the faint glow of the night-light, he feasted his eyes on the delightful curves and smooth contours of her body, then he lay down beside her. Careful not to wake her, he traced his fingertips lightly over her breasts and stomach, marvelling at the warm, velvety feel of her skin. He pressed his face closer, enjoying the sweet, clean scent of her, then he tasted her with his tongue. Gently he brushed his lips against her cheek and she stirred in her sleep. He lay perfectly still for a few moments, then he kissed her tenderly once more and whispered, 'I love you, little rose. I always will.'

She kept her eyes closed and waited until his breathing was deep and even, then she turned, laid her head on his chest and listened to the steady beat of his heart. 'And I'll always love you, my beautiful barbarian,' she whispered.

With a smile of blissful contentment on her face, she closed her eyes and fell asleep.

**BRIDE'S BAY RESORT**

## UNLOCK THE DOOR TO GREAT ROMANCE AT BRIDE'S BAY RESORT

Join Harlequin's new across-the-lines series, set in an exclusive hotel on an island off the coast of South Carolina.

Seven of your favorite authors will bring you exciting stories about fascinating heroes and heroines discovering love at Bride's Bay Resort.

Look for these fabulous stories coming to a store near you beginning in January 1996.

**Harlequin American Romance #613 in January**
*Matchmaking Baby* by Cathy Gillen Thacker

**Harlequin Presents #1794 in February**
*Indiscretions* by Robyn Donald

**Harlequin Intrigue #362 in March**
*Love and Lies* by Dawn Stewardson

**Harlequin Romance #3404 in April**
*Make Believe Engagement* by Day Leclaire

**Harlequin Temptation #588 in May**
*Stranger in the Night* by Roseanne Williams

**Harlequin Superromance #695 in June**
*Married to a Stranger* by Connie Bennett

**Harlequin Historicals #324 in July**
*Dulcie's Gift* by Ruth Langan

Visit Bride's Bay Resort each month wherever Harlequin books are sold.

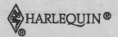

**HARLEQUIN ®**

BBAYG

# HARLEQUIN PRESENTS®

brings you

*Second Honeymoon*
by
*Sandra Field*

The second book in her great new series,
*Significant Others*. A series that celebrates the magical
mayhem of modern relationships and follows the loves,
lives and passionate adventures of Lucy Barnes and
her sister Marcia.

In *Beyond Reach*, Lucy was a happy bride—now she's
a runaway wife! Could her estranged husband,
Troy Donovan, be just the guy to catch her? Lucy has
turned her back on love—it hurts too much. It's hardly
an invitation for a second honeymoon, but Troy needs his
wife back or out of his system for good. He's determined
to get what he wants—even if it means seducing his
own wife....

**The exciting sequel to *Beyond Reach!***

"Sandra Field pens a phenomenal love story...
pure pleasure."                  *—Romantic Times*

**Sandra Field's page-turning new trilogy:**

*First they were strangers, then they were lovers, now
they're Significant Others!*

by Charlotte Lamb

An exciting seven-part series.

Watch for

**The Sin of Envy**

in

**#1828 HAUNTED DREAMS**

Ambrose Kerr possessed the kind of wealth and success
others could only dream about—but his happiness would
not be complete until he had Emilie!

*Love can conquer the deadliest of*

HARLEQUIN 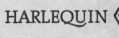 PRESENTS®

Available in August wherever Harlequin books are sold.

Look us up on-line at: http://www.romance.net

SINS3